# CHILDREN OF THE MIRACLE

## DANIEL WEISBECK

**Publisher, Copyright, and Additional Information**

*Children of the Miracle* by Daniel Weisbeck published by DJW Books,
www.danielweisbeckbooks.com

ISBN: 978-1-5272-6150-1

Cover design and interior design by Rafael Andres

# CHAPTER ONE

The capital lobby hummed with the usual daily business and orderly activities of visitors with appointments. Government workers steadily appeared on the quarter-hour, dressed in the red uniforms of junior staff, and collected the waiting citizens, shuffling them back down the dark hallways from which they arrived. No visitors, however, were being ushered through the large metal doors emblazoned with the words HIGH CHAMBER.

Sitting in the lobby, hands knitted tightly together, Mercy Perching anxiously bounced her knee while she waited. Odd, but not unexpected was her conclusion on the urgent meeting from the Leaders of the Sanctuary. They must have read her report on the resistance gene offering immunity to the virus, she told herself. Their request was sooner than she had anticipated, but even the slightest possibility of a cure would explain their insistence.

Mercy twisted her fingers white. She would be succinct in her presentation, she told herself. She would not repeat the things they already knew, like one hundred years after the pandemic, they still did not have a vaccine. Or that synthetic antidotes had failed. No, today was about hope. Her research opened up a new door of possibilities, and Mercy had to convince them to let her continue her work.

A sudden loud mechanical clank quieted the soft conversations in the lobby. All eyes were on the large metal doors to the High Chamber as they slid smoothly sideways; one to the left and one to the right. Two officers flanking the entrance in perfectly cut sapphire blue uniforms decorated with the military insignia of a wheat shaft crossed over by a sword, stood to attention.

'Doctor Mercy Perching!' trumpeted one of the guards.

Mercy rose from the bench to stares and whispers from onlookers and gossip herders who were eager to guess at her importance.

'Isn't that the Director of the Department of Population Reclamation?' one asked.

'Yes. She's working on a vaccine,' answered someone from behind.

'She's so young,' said another.

Fair of skin and hair, able-bodied, and taller than most, Mercy already stood out. But her one hazel eye and the other muddy blue set her apart from all others.

'Amazing!' declared her Doctor on nearly every visit. His torch zigzagged from one pupil to the other. 'Heterochromia. Completely different coloured eyes. So rare. You're a genetic miracle.'

'There are no miracles, Doctor. Only science,' Mercy would reply, shaking her head at the old man's lack of respect for genetics.

If she had inherited this unique feature from her parents, she wouldn't have known. A child of the Population Reclamation Program, her life had started in a lab: fertilised in a test tube, carried by an unknown surrogate, and raised by the government to fulfil the Sanctuary's aggressive, but not impossible, population growth targets.

Mercy entered the High Chamber. A sudden stillness muted the busy employees and chattering citizens outside. The scent of old stone and cedar wood permeated the large room. Rows of hanging pendants cast halos of soft light on the marbled floors, illuminating a path down the long hall. At the far end of the room, behind an elevated judges' bench, five officials of eminence, adorned in red scarlet robes with starched white neckings, sat talking among themselves. If they noticed her entrance, they gave no sign.

Mercy approached the bench with a wordless reverence commanded by the Leaders' seniority. The click, click, click of her shoes against the polished floor was the only sound she dared make until sanctioned to speak.

There were no seats for those given an audience in the High Chamber, standing implied a limited expectancy of allowed time. Mercy took her position in front of the waist-high metal piling that rose from the ground at the foot of the altar – both a podium for presenting and a holographic display at once.

On the far right of the bench sat a thin-faced man known as the Fifth, the most senior of the Leaders. His pale skin hung loosely over his protruding skull bones like wet paper. His was the job of welcoming and commencing business.

'Doctor Perching, thank you for coming in person today.'

Mercy offered a polite bow. 'Thank you for granting me the audience. I know your time is valuable.'

'We,' he waved his hand to the right, fluidly pointing to the other four leaders flanking him; three women and one man, 'read your recent report on the FossilFlu immunity project with interest. I understand you've made some progress?'

'Yes, Leaders,' Mercy said, privately pleased they had understood the importance of her research. She placed a hand over the round podium in front of her, triggering a shaft of light to jet upward until disappearing into the ether of the room. A translucent image of a DNA strand materialised and hung in the air waiting for an explanation.

'I've spent the last two years studying the descendants of the host carcass which released FossilFlu during the polar melt. Based on the age of the fossil, I believe our evolutionary ancestors were exposed to the virus for many years, even thousands. In that time, they could have evolved a virus resistance gene, making them immune. If my theory is right, humans could also carry the gene.

'As we are the only species which were infected by the virus outbreak, it could be that the gene is silenced. To prove my theory, we had first to confirm the existence of a viral resistance gene in mammals. And last week we had a breakthrough.'

The Leaders leaned into the bench, eyebrows raised. Mercy zoomed in on the holographic DNA strand and pulled out a microscopic section until large and easily visible. The isolated string of nodules glowed.

'I'm very pleased to be able to share with the Council that the immunity gene does exist,' Mercy declared proudly. 'This is the virus-induced gene that is responsible for mammalian resistance to the FossilFlu.'

The Fifth's eyes widened with interest, but he held back any outspoken enthusiasm. Mercy was aware that many scientists before her had tried and failed to find the cure for FossilFlu. The Council's hesitation was expected.

The Third, her role being security and defence of the Sanctuary, a woman of more flesh but equal in years to the Fifth, leaned back into her chair and crossed her arms. 'I would like to congratulate you, Doctor. Your discovery is ground-breaking work. But, I'm curious about your next steps. How exactly does this help humans if our immunity gene is silenced?'

Mercy drew a deep breath and squared her shoulders in anticipation of their response. She had rehearsed this moment in her mind many times, and many times they had applauded and thanked her, and many more they had looked down on her in shock and horror and cried for her head.

'As we have yet to find a vaccine to FossilFlu, I propose it's time we take a more aggressive approach. With the Leaders permission, I would like to try genetically modifying the human genome with animal DNA. Inserting the active resistance gene sequence to replace our own,' answered Mercy, hiding her anxiety behind a confident face.

There was a heavy silence. Mercy's heart leapt into her throat. She wanted to race on, explain more about the procedure or her hypothesis, to explain that her computer simulations showed it was possible. Yet, something held her back. They had not jumped out of their chairs in outrage. They had not labelled her a maverick or a mad scientist. No, she told herself, stay calm and let them make the next move.

The Leaders turned away, huddled at the centre of the bench, and spoke in a low private tone among themselves. Mercy strained but failed to make out words or intent.

The Fifth broke the silence. 'Doctor Perching, what we are about to tell you may come as a surprise, even a shock. This information must remain in the strictest confidence.'

Mercy squinted her eyes, cautious. 'Yes.'

'We have reason to believe others may have already reached this conclusion in their research.'

'Others?' she asked in a quiet voice.

'Yes. The Sanctuary of Americas.'

'Who?' She stared in wild-eyed bewilderment. Up until this moment, like all the citizens of the Sanctuary of Europe, Mercy believed they were the last humans on the planet.

The Fifth went on: 'The Sanctuary of Europe was not the only Sanctuary to survive the global pandemic. There were two others: the Sanctuary of Americas and the Sanctuary of Asia. Of course, our ancestors didn't know this at first.

'After the pandemic, when the risk of infection was deemed low enough, the Sanctuary's Leaders sent out scouts to see if any other humans were alive. They assumed the worse. But they were wrong. Others did survive, living isolated in Sanctuary cities like ours.

'It should have been a time of hope. Unfortunately, the first contact between Sanctuaries resulted in tensions. Scarce resources led to accusations of stealing, spying, and fear of invasions. In the interest of avoiding a possible war, all contact between the Sanctuaries ended. For our protection, each Sanctuary has continued to remain isolated.'

The Fifth's demeanour changed. His face softened, and his shoulders relaxed. 'This burden, keeping the lie, is something every Council of Leaders has had to carry over the last one hundred years. And now, Doctor Perching, I am sorry, but it's a burden you will have to carry as well.'

Mercy stared into the blinding headlights of an alternative reality. She was getting more and more confused the longer she thought about it. If the citizens of the Sanctuary found out there were other survivors; it would change everything. Solidarity was the foundation of their society; to survive together, to repopulate the Earth together, to build a new planet together. Learning that others existed, would seed mistrust in the government and create chaos. No, she told herself, this could not be the truth – not the truth they could afford to share.

'Doctor Perching, do you understand?' asked the Fifth, seeking a response.

'I do,' she finally answered, even though understanding didn't lessen the shock.

The Third Leader continued from the Fifth. 'Last week we received a message from the Sanctuary of Americas. The message was brief. They have encountered a mutation of the FossilFlu. A more deadly strain that infects both animals and humans alike.'

'What? How?' Mercy exclaimed. 'Are they sure it's the same virus? Is it spreading?' Her questions were rapid, formulated; a doctor's response.

'The message didn't clarify anything further on the virus other than to reassure us they have it contained, for now.'

The Fifth interrupted, 'We've also received a second message, from an unknown source. It claims the Sanctuary of Americas has been running genetic experiments combining human and animal DNA seeking a cure to FossilFlu. Exactly as you requested here today. The unknown source suggests this is the host the virus needed to mutate.'

Mercy's lifetime of research into FossilFlu flashed before her. The excitement of her discovery. The hope for a future cure. All of it put in doubt, possibly gone forever. Her reaction must have been evident to the leaders.

The Fifth counselled, 'I'm sure this news is disappointing. But for now, we need to focus on the greater problem – the impact this could have if the virus started spreading again. The ability of the mutation to kill both animals and humans would mean the extinction of all life. What little remains.'

'You said they closed their borders to us years ago out of mistrust. Why contact us now?' Mercy asked.

The Third continued, 'We've known they monitor us…'

The First Leader, his role being information and communication, interrupted, 'Spy on us, you mean.'

The Third glanced at him out of the corner of her eye and pinched her lips, scolding. 'Yes, the video is rather overt regarding their intelligence and how up to date it is.' She reluctantly agreed with him. 'In short, they contacted us to get to you and your research.'

'Me?' Mercy felt her knees go weak. 'I don't understand. How can they know about my research?'

The Third answered humbly, 'We don't have answers to that yet. More importantly, having received the two messages from different sources tells us something more is going on. We can't assume they are telling the entire truth about the outbreak.'

'I'm sorry, but I still don't understand what I can do?' questioned Mercy.

The Fifth spoke for the bench. 'Their offer is an exchange. You travel to the Sanctuary of Americas, share your research, and work with their scientists, and, if collaboration is successful, we all share the cure.'

Before Mercy could ask any more questions, the mood in the room shifted. The Third leaned in, aggressive, asserting her authority. 'Doctor Perching, is it true that you have no partner or plans to surrogate? So, nothing significant holding you back?'

'Yes, that's right,' she conceded, a bit bruised. Population regeneration being the responsibility of all citizens.

'Good. I hope you understand why we called you here today, and what we are asking of you?'

There could be no mistaking their request to accept the invitation.

'When would I go?' Mercy asked.

'You'll go into briefing today and leave for the Sanctuary of Americas tomorrow.' Her answer blunt, not offering negotiations. 'It's better for all if you disappear quickly to avoid any possible leaks.'

'My team…'

'We'll take care of the communication.'

A man, unseen before, crept from the shadows of the chamber, startling Mercy. He wore the red felt bodysuit of the Council's cabinet. His jet-black hair, braided and tied back, and his youthful, muscular form were a stark and pleasant contrast to the withered flesh behind the alter. The emblematic Phoenix clasping a wheat shaft and a rod pinned to his chest, the national symbol of the Sanctuary, indicated his status as a direct agent of the Leaders. He approached the bench and stopped, waiting for his introduction.

'This is Agent Basil. He will be your person of contact going forward. He will brief you on the mission details over the next twenty-four hours if you accept,' outlined the Third.

The Fifth made the final plea. 'Doctor Perching, I won't lie. Once you cross the border into their Sanctuary, there is little protection we can offer. I can only ask that you consider the survival of our Sanctuary, perhaps the survival of humanity. Will you help us?'

Mercy's mind swirled with questions and doubts. The Five Leaders peered down at her expectantly, unflinching.

After an extended silence, tolerated more than granted, she nodded, offering the Leaders the only answer she knew they would accept. 'Yes, I will do what I can.'

# CHAPTER TWO

Spellbound Mercy gazed at the endless silver and blue ocean rising and falling in rhythmic swells below her. The drone's propellers, barely audible, whirred continuously. The brails on the end of the gold-foil sail swayed east in the headwind as she followed the Forty-Fifth Parallel north on her way to the Sanctuary of Americas. Any further near the equator and she risked entering the Red Zone, an area that had grown too hot for life and electronic motors.

Children of the Sanctuary learned of the ocean through historical archives and ancient stories of mythical creatures. The risk of another epidemic meant only military and miners were allowed beyond the city's walls. Having never seen it for themselves, the stories of monsters were as real as any video archive. The truth, however, proved much more terrifying. Overfishing and rising water temperatures long ago left most animal life in the oceans severely diminished if not eradicated. Other than the occasional small school of tiny krill, squids and siphonophores, sightings of fish or large sea creatures were not to be expected.

Knowing all of this, Mercy still studied the lifeless void with a child's anticipation, waiting for the ocean to come alive. Shadows rippling below the surface could be a whale, reflections of the sun on distant waves seabirds, only to be revealed as nothing more than mirages up close.

'Agent Basil is requesting a call,' interrupted Gia's voice from the ship's helm.

To Mercy's relief, Gia had been upgraded to captain the ship. Her Personal Virtual Assistant (PVA) since childhood, Gia was a database of everything she had ever done. More than an assistant, she was a teacher, confidant and advisor. Gia was as close to family as Mercy had come. Hearing her voice always brought comfort.

'Accept Agent Basil's call,' answered Mercy.

After forty-eight hours with Agent Basil, Mercy had come to like the man. Both of them young, and already accomplished in their careers, neither dominated the other. His briefing was well laid out, and he always gave room for her questions – of which there were many. Within the short period, he covered the mission's objectives, the protocols she would be expected to follow as a representative of the Sanctuary of Europe, and what little information they had about the Sanctuary of Americas.

'When you arrive at the shoreline, you'll be greeted outside a shield that protects the entire Sanctuary territory. It's impressive,' Agent Basil had told her. The excitement rising in his voice was a rare break from his usual studied manner. 'The force field is constructed of picotechnology. Airborne atomic particles with the ability to communicate through artificial intelligence, making the field flexible. We believe the shield blocks harmful solar radiation while also harvesting the sun's energy and converting it into electricity. The magnetic field blocks all inward-bound surveillance, which is why we know less about them than they do about us. The technology in parts isn't beyond our reach, but the sheer scale of what they have achieved is impressive. The force field must be covering a landmass area of over one million square miles.'

Agent Basil's briefing also covered the unofficial roles.

'Doctor Perching, as the first citizen of the Sanctuary to cross into the field, we will be very interested in your observations.'

She understood the request. More than a doctor, more than an emissary – her job was the watcher of all things: a snoop.

A miniature hologram of Agent Basil appeared above the helm's communicator.

'Good day, Doctor Perching. I trust everything is going as expected?'

'As expected? Considering I don't know exactly what I'm going to be doing and I'm heading to a country I didn't even know existed? Probably; most likely as expected,' she quipped.

'The council has asked that I express their appreciation again for your willingness and sacrifice.' He assured her.

'Sacrifice?' Her voice was slightly concerned.

'Trust that your safety is paramount for us.'

'Hmm,' she grunted half-heartedly. 'Reassuring considering it's coming from the same people who just revealed they've been telling a one-hundred-year lie.'

One side of the Agent's lips reluctantly curled into a half-smile. 'Yes, well, a lie you're at the heart of now. It's important to remember this is as much a diplomatic trip as it is scientific. Your every word and action will be interpreted as coming from the Council of Leaders. We need to ensure the people of the Sanctuary of Americas understand we come with goodwill and a desire to build a long-term relationship.'

His words reminded her once again how ill-prepared she felt for this mission. Politics and being the centre of attention were not her strengths. Mercy should have been sitting in a lab behind the white barrels of microscopes and never-ending streams of data. She had to push her doubts aside. Give them too much room, and she might turn around.

'As a reminder, once you approach the force field, you will be greeted by a representative of their President, Ambassador Joan. She will escort you through the shield and into the city. At that point, our only communication will be one-way video recordings that they will send back and forth on our behalf.'

'Yes – a strange requirement for an open invitation, isn't it?'

'It's been nearly a hundred years since contact. I'm sure they will want to monitor your communication for sensitive information, even if they have assured us they won't filter the messages. I do think it would be prudent if we agreed on a safe word if you need help, though.'

Mercy thought for a short while. 'My tree.'

'Excuse me?'

'The tree in my apartment.'

Mercy's apartment back in the Sanctuary was meagrely decorated, but compliant with her living and dining requirements. There were no personal artefacts to be seen; no pictures on the walls, no books on shelves, no favourite knick-knacks or ornaments dotted around. It's not that she wanted her home to be impersonal, she just didn't see the point, spending most of her days and nights in the lab. However, her one personal transgression was a small stunted orange tree, illegally kept, as any use of water in the Sanctuary was heavily regulated and for essential purposes only.

'How about if I ask you to remember to water my tree?' Mercy offered.

He paused. 'Well, now that I'm complicit in your crime, thank you,' he teased, 'I believe that should be innocuous enough. Yes, let's use that.'

'Good. But really, do remember to water my tree.'

'Consider it done. Be safe. Our hopes are with you.'

Just as Agent Basil was about to sign off, Mercy jolted from her seat. A shadowy form, deep in the water, appeared beneath her.

'Is something wrong?' asked Agent Basil, not yet evaporated.

'Something is under the ship! Something huge, in the water,' she cried out, her eyes locked on the living silhouette moving towards her.

'Ah, yes. I can see the ship's sensors have identified the object as organic. It's likely a whale at that size. Our navy has spotted them occasionally, but only out in the deep, far away from land. Take it as a good omen, Doctor Perching.'

Mercy quickly signed off. With a blink, Agent Basil disappeared.

'Gia, can you identify the object?' Mercy asked excitedly.

'It appears to be a Blue whale. A near-extinct species.'

The whale slipped under their ship. Mercy's heart raced. A strange urge took her by surprise, bypassing a perpetual sense of responsibility – it felt like rebellion.

'Gia, turn around, lock in on the whale and follow along.'

'This is outside our protocol, Mercy. Agent Basil will have to be notified.'

'It's only for a moment. He'll understand.'

The gold-foil sails spun round, turning the ship about-face. Within minutes, they were riding the bow of the enormous creature. Mercy gazed unflinchingly at the black image weaving through the undulating water canopy when suddenly the great beast, all thirty metres of flesh, began to surface, water sweeping down its rubbery skin. A feathery plume of water shot out of the hole atop its head. Mercy gasped with delight and ordered Gia to descend as they came to swim with the whale, at its side, hovering vertically. A solitary eye, human-like, watched them, curious.

'Mercy, Agent Basil is asking for an update on our change of course,' interrupted Gia.

Mercy, transfixed, couldn't bring herself to break the mystical connection; the whale would have to be the first to leave. Then, almost as if it sensed her dilemma, the whale sank weightlessly below the water's surface. With incredible agility, it turned full face and started swimming in the opposite direction, towards the Sanctuary of Americas.

'We do understand each other,' whispered Mercy under her breath, giddy with excitement. 'Gia, how long can we follow the whale and still reach the Sanctuary on time?'

'Headwinds are low. At this speed, we will arrive at the Sanctuary ahead of schedule.'

'Great. Tell Agent Basil we are on our way to the Sanctuary and follow behind the whale until we need to get back on course.'

In what felt like only a minute, thirty had passed. The animal's freedom caught at Mercy. Something of the vastness of the open ocean and the effortless speed of the rare giant gliding below her brought a calm respite from the terrifying job ahead of her.

*So, this is the power of nature. To feel small, but not alone. To feel connected, but also free. This is what we've lost*, she thought sadly.

Gia broke the silence. 'Mercy, we've shifted eighty-six knots north off-course following the whale. However, we can still arrive ahead of schedule if we correct course now.'

Mercy ignored her.

*Why did you change course after our encounter? Was it just a coincidence? Did you want to be followed?*

'Gia, run a calculation on the whale's path forward in a straight line and scan satellite images between here and the Sanctuary of Americas. Let me know if there is anything other than water.'

'Images show an uninhabited volcanic island around one hundred kilometres from our current location in due course with the whale's path. Otherwise, the satellite shows only open ocean until we reach the Sanctuary of Americas,' relayed Gia.

'One hundred kilometres? Is that all? We can certainly sneak a visit and still meet the Ambassador on time. Gia, change course for a quick flyover of the island and let's pick up the pace.'

'Another change in course will need to be explained to Agent Basil.'

'Fine, share our destination. Report the reason for the detour as scientific research.'

Plumes of grey smoke billowed high into the air, breaking the monotonous azure skyline. A solitary black rock mountain rose up and out of the horizon as they sped forward, revealing itself as the source of the stuttering ash clouds teasing to erupt at any moment. Isolated, the volcano cut a haunting image against the vacant landscape. The loneliness reverberated through Mercy. She longed for the whale they had left behind, wishing they had arrived together.

*What is it you wanted to show me?* She asked again.

'Gia, how close can we get to the island?'

'Ten kilometres away from the volcano's vent and staying upwind of the plume puts us in a safe zone.'

'Understood. Fly around the island once and then let's head out,' she relinquished, ready to give up on her adventure.

The volcano's western precipice, three-hundred-foot sheer cliffs, was bald and wind-swept, beaten by ceaseless crashing ocean waves erupting into fountains of sea spray and swirling foam. Its eastern front, in contrast, was a long undulating terrain with a serrated spine flanked on each side by a rib cage of eroding gullies sloping downward into shallow beaches.

The lifeless island, tranquilising for all its volatility and anger bubbling inside, offered no clues why it might be a destination of choice on first sight. Then, unexpectedly, under the rippling day's heat, reflecting off the black-glass sand beach, she spotted a trespasser, something white and substantial.

'Gia, use cameras to zoom in on the beach.'

An image appeared on the glass windshield through which Mercy stared with awe. Bones. Hundreds of them. Rows upon rows of skeletons. Giant arches of sun-bleached rib cages and skull boulders.

The island's coast was a boneyard of beached whales. Mercy had heard stories of mass animal graveyards that appeared during the early stages of the environmental crisis, mostly caused by land mammals migrating to water sources only to find dry lakes and riverbeds. But this didn't explain why these whales came together to die. Her initial excitement suddenly slipped away.

*Is this why you changed course? Are you coming to die?*

She couldn't wait around for the answers. A pressing sense of lateness and obligation forced her to move on.

'Gia, scan the whale skeletons' cellular structures, collect photos and let's head out to meet the Ambassador.'

Mercy left the island and the whale behind, hoping her new friend might never find this place.

# CHAPTER THREE

'The shield that protects the Sanctuary of Americas is now visible,' reported Gia dutifully.

Mercy scanned the horizon anxiously as they arrived at the coordinates where they were scheduled to meet the Ambassador. The rapid succession of events that had brought her to this point left her little time to imagine much about the Sanctuary of Americas. However, what confronted her provided more questions than answers. Emptiness filled the skyline for as far as Mercy could see. The barrier's edge, a reflectionless veil like a dense fog, offered no hint of what lay on the other side.

Mercy waited. 'Gia, are you sure we've arrived in the right location?'

On cue, appearing out of thin air, the nose of a flying ship slowly broke through the surface of the shield. Once entirely through the barrier, the object revealed itself as a solid metallic sphere with no windows, jets, propellers, or sails. The egg-shaped vehicle came to a stop, hovering.

'The Ambassador is hailing us,' Gia alerted.

Mercy tugged at the hem of her white jacket, pulling it tight. She briefly touched the silver badge pinned to her coat, the national symbol of the Sanctuary of Europe, reminding her of the mission and duty to the Leaders.

'Put them through, Gia.' Her command was confident.

'Hello, Doctor Perching,' said a young woman hovering over her ships helm.

The severity of the Ambassador's appearance – a perfectly tailored blue military uniform, stiff posture, hair as white as snow pulled tightly back into a bun, and stoic expression – seemed an effort to downplay her exceptional beauty. The woman's extraordinarily large dark round eyes and smooth porcelain skin struck Mercy as exaggerated, almost too perfect.

'Hello, Ambassador Joan,' Mercy replied. 'It's a pleasure to meet you.'

'On behalf of the Prime, I'd like to welcome you to the Sanctuary of Americas,' the Ambassador said, breaking into a friendly smile. 'I'll be your escort on this trip. I trust your travels went well?'

'Yes, thank you. I'm sorry, the Prime?' questioned Mercy, with no knowledge of the title.

Ambassador Joan tilted her head quizzically. 'My apologies,' she offered, suddenly understanding Mercy's confusion. 'The Prime is the name given to our leader elect. She runs the Sanctuary of Americas. You probably referred to the role of our President-elect. We haven't used that title for a very long time,' she explained.

Mercy wondered why Agent Basil hadn't included this information in her briefing and how many more surprises lay ahead.

The Ambassador continued, 'Not to worry, Doctor; it's my job to acquaint you with our civilisation.'

*Civilisation?* Mercy squinted her eyes at the sound of it. Odd, she thought. City, nation, even culture seemed more appropriate considering their shared past.

'Thank you, Ambassador,' Mercy continued in a practiced tone. 'The Leaders of the Sanctuary of Europe hope this will be a fruitful and long-lasting relationship between our cities. We only regret that it's come under these circumstances.'

The Ambassador nodded sympathetically. 'Your Leaders speak very highly of you and your research into the FossilFlu. Our scientists have made some progress as well and are anxious to meet you.'

A slight blush quickly faded from Mercy's cheeks. 'I look forward to working with them.'

The Ambassador nodded to someone on her ship outside of the hologram.

'You've likely noticed the shield over the Sanctuary through which we arrived,' she continued addressing Mercy. 'We call this the Shade. Unfortunately, you won't be able to take your ship further for security reasons. From this point on, you'll be travelling with us. My colleague has sent your PVA the coordinates of a stationary naval ship nearby. It can dock there until your return. I apologise, but your PVA will need to remain with your ship as well. Will this be okay?'

'Certainly. I understand,' Mercy answered, hiding her surprise. A sudden and unexpected panic arrested her. She had never been without access to Gia. Ashamed of the childish fear, she pushed it aside.

'I'm sending the docking bay out to retrieve you now. We'll see you on our ship, Doctor Perching.' The Ambassador signed off, her image evaporating to silence.

Through her windshield, Mercy watched in astonishment as a liquid metal bubble squirted itself out of the side of the Ambassador's ship. The blob rolled out into a disk-like platform, hovering over the ocean without any visible engine. The platform jetted towards her vehicle.

'Gia, relay the port coordinates to Agent Basil and inform him you will not be joining me. Also, send images of the Ambassador's ship and the transport platform. He'll love this. And while you port on the Sanctuary's ship, please remain in confidential mode. Do not allow correspondence with anyone on the docking ship.'

'Yes, understood. Mercy?'

'Yes?'

'I believe one says good luck at this point.'

'That's correct. I'm going to need a lot of luck.'

Mercy slipped on a full-body cape and pulled the protective hood over her head as the hatch on her ship opened. A burst of hot air shot at her cloak and whipped her hair repeatedly against her face as she clutched her hood. Cautiously stepping onto the hovercraft docked outside her ship, a gravitational pull locked her feet steadily onto its surface.

Slowly, the platform, nothing more than a thin sliver of metal stopping her from a death spiral into the white-capped ocean below, levitated her back to the Ambassador's ship. For all the wind and bluster of the outside world, the hovercraft remained remarkably stable.

Approaching the Ambassador's shuttle, Mercy could find no hint of a hatch or opening. Out of nowhere, a ripple began to form on the surface of the metal sphere. The rings expanded and increased in frequency outward until the thinning liquid stretched effortlessly into an open doorway, revealing Ambassador Joan standing opposite. She gestured for Mercy to enter. The floating platform retracted its gravitational hold, and Mercy stepped on board, into the Sanctuary of Americas itself.

Mercy blinked twice with astonishment. Other than the floor, the ship's hull, opaque from the outside, had mysteriously become transparent when standing inside, offering unrestricted views of the ocean and sky.

Ambassador Joan presented her hand. 'Welcome on board, Doctor Perching.'

'Thank you,' Mercy accepted.

Their touch gave Mercy a start, and she had to fight off an instinct to recoil. A sheath of short, barely visible white hair – soft, like the hairs on a newborn baby's head, and dense like fur, covered the back of the Ambassador's hand.

Mercy was quick to feign an even broader, almost silly, smile to avoid a reaction that might offend the Ambassador.

The Ambassador continued unfazed. 'This is Private Theo,' she waved a hand towards a young man stood at the ship's helm. His snow-white hair, close-cropped, and pearl-smooth rounded face, bore such a striking similarity to the Ambassador they could have been twins.

'Hello,' Mercy nodded his way.

The soldier gave a courteous smile and returned to his seat in front of the navigation panels, readied for travel.

'Please, Doctor Perching,' requested Ambassador Joan, pointing to the chair directly behind hers. 'We'll get going. The Prime will be meeting us at the White Tower shortly.'

The metal sphere jetted smoothly forward. Mercy caught sight of her ship and Gia, already far in the distance, slipping away. *No turning back now*, she thought as she sighed privately.

# CHAPTER FOUR

The Ambassador's ship glided into the Shade without resistance. Mercy got the impression of a light switch being turned off and then immediately on again as they passed through the shadow wall. On the other side, the sky returned to the same, bright, azure blue as the world outside its barrier. In every direction, the Shade had become invisible.

Something in the distance caught Mercy's eye. There was a movement in the sky directly ahead of them. As the ship sped forward, the undistinguished arrows took shape, revealing hundreds of seabirds soaring through the air. Mercy jutted her body forward in her seat, wide-eyed. She wanted to call out the sighting as if it were her discovery. However, the unstirred passengers in front of her quickly hampered her naive excitement. She drew back into her chair and forced her body to sit quietly.

Flocks of white-feathered seabirds with black-lined wings and golden beaks floated on unseen currents, effortlessly stationary until turning sharply on their axis and one by one plunge-diving into the water towards a dark shadow rising.

Below the ship's helm, at the birds' target, rings of effervescent bubbles surfaced first, followed immediately by a swirling hive of anchovies. Millions of silver slivers endlessly shape-shifted like an underwater tornado, continually pushing and testing the invisible bubble net.

A rambunctious pool of dolphins suddenly shot up from the shadowy depths. Using their bodies as a lasso, they held the perimeters tight and pushed the swarm further up to the surface.

Within minutes, hungry interlopers appeared, ready for a feast. A frenzied congregation of birds, sharks and seals joined the dolphins, splitting the pool of fish thinner and thinner while pecking away at the edges.

Ambassador Joan turned in her chair, facing Mercy.

'Truly amazing,' enthused Mercy, shaking her head in bewilderment.

'Yes, we're getting close to land. You'll start to see a lot more wildlife.'

'We were taught that the sea was dead,' shared Mercy with the same sadness the citizens of Europe always used when talking about the state of the world outside the Sanctuary.

'A lot has changed since we worked together,' offered the Ambassador, an introduction to Mercy's first lesson on the Sanctuary of Americas. 'The Shade is essentially a weather-control machine. It allows us to modify solar radiation and atmospheric gases, even control weather patterns down to the metre. It's at the heart of our land and sea reclamation project, which consists of seven different biomes surrounding Sanctuary City. Each biotic unit has different plant and animal ecosystems. While we are far from complete, the reclamation project has already brought thousands of extinct species back from the Scorch.'

'The Scorch,' smiled Mercy, repeating the Ambassador's use of the word.

'Excuse me?'

'You called it the Scorch. We use the same term for the environmental collapse.'

'Ah, yes,' nodded the Ambassador, acknowledging a shared past.


A silhouette unmistakable as land emerged over the Ambassador's shoulders. The thin shadow on the horizon between the ocean and sky slowly expanded out and upward as they approached.

Reaching the dry edge of the sea, a long-untouched crystal-white beach, Mercy witnessed something beyond any expectations. The skyline was filled with a vibrant tropical rainforest. Trees, in abundance, as far as the eye could see. The giant palms and lush undergrowth stretched across the length and depth of the horizon.

'It's so green...' blurted Mercy, unable to hold back her excitement.

'This is the beginning of the Green Belt,' explained the Ambassador. 'The Belt is a ring that follows our coastline around the continent, moving inland to the Sanctuary City. We keep it free of human habitation, giving nature a chance to thrive. We are passing over the east side of the Belt, a tropical rainforest.

'Our west coast is a desert. Not the dead landscapes of the Scorch, mind you,' she said with a note of pride in her voice. 'This desert has up to one million different species of plants and animals.

'The southern biome is primarily grasslands and marshes leading to a thriving coral reef off the coast.

'And the north is our glacial mountain range covered in pine and boreal forests. The tip of the north coast hosts an arctic tundra.'

'You have snow?' Mercy asked in shock.

The Ambassador smiled. 'Yes. Weather patterns follow four seasonal changes, synchronised through all the biomes: summer, autumn, winter, and spring.'

The idea of having seasons and water in all forms – rain, snow, and ice – seemed a downright fantasy to Mercy.

The Ambassador commanded Theo to slow the ship and open a sky port, leaving a gaping hole to the outside world directly over their heads. She produced a small red pill and handed it to Mercy. 'You'll need to take this,' instructed the Ambassador.

'What is it?'

'Even though the Shade regulates solar radiation to levels acceptable for human exposure, you've been sheltered inside too long. Your skin is much more sensitive than ours. The pill will help protect you and make sure you don't get a sunburn.'

*Sunburn.* The relaxed tone in which the Ambassador said it struck Mercy as sacrilegious; as if she were simply warning her to watch her step over a small crack in the floor. Exposing oneself to the sun for an extended time, intentionally, was sheer lunacy in the Sanctuary of Europe and would result in days of radiation treatments to avoid malignant cellular formations.

Mercy swallowed the pill. 'How long before it takes effect?'

'Almost instantly. You can already stand up if you like.'

Unsure, but drawn, Mercy stood under the opening. A chilly air kissed her skin – and something else, something she couldn't immediately identify. Placing a hand on her cheek, she held back a fit of laughter. 'Wet. The air is wet!' Mercy exclaimed.

With closed eyes, her face glowing with rapture, she breathed deeply, greedily, allowing the moisture deep into her lungs. Something in her bones yawned awake from an old memory, older than her flesh. Again, she breathed deeper and longer. Her hand reached up into the crisp air and bright sunshine, washing away a lifetime of dust and darkness.

At a sudden disturbance, she opened her eyes. The air had changed. A pressure was building in her head as a low metallic purr tickled her ears. She closed her eyes again, shook her head, and opened them once more. The noise was real, and it was coming from outside the ship. The deep bass drumming, reverberating in waves, grew louder and louder.

'What's happening?' she cried.

Before the Ambassador could answer, mayhem exploded beneath her feet. Treetops bent and swayed against a sudden wind, followed by a cacophony of screeching bird calls erupting from the forest. Hundreds of feathered living things shot out of the canopy up into the air. They circled and dove and rose again in a frenzy.

Mercy, wild-eyed and terrified, turned to the Ambassador who, to her surprise, was smiling. Neither the Ambassador nor Private Theo appeared to be worried; in fact, they seemed to be enjoying themselves. With a heavy sigh of relief and a borrowed sense of comfort, Mercy calmed herself.

Beneath her, the forest continued to shiver against a growing gale wind, waking the rest of its residents. Right on cue, as if a conductor had swung his baton, the birds were joined in the celebration by an entire forest of animals. Howls, barks, roars and snorts rose from beneath the impenetrable arbour until living noise rivalled the inorganic drumming overhead.

A flash of light caught Mercy from the side of her eye, immediately followed by a head-splitting crack, giving her the sensation of a shock. The hair on the back of her neck and arms stood. She jumped at the noise, letting out a squeal. In the direction of the boom, puffs and streaks of white appeared out of thin air. Clouds were rapidly building in the sky. Underneath their shadowy cover, an arch of colours suddenly glowed, stretching across the entire horizon.

'Is that a rainbow?' yelled Mercy over the noise, never having seen one before.

Joan raised her eyebrows and nodded, smiling.

Something cold and wet slapped against Mercy's face, then another thing, and suddenly millions more. The rain started to pour down in sheets. Theo quickly closed the portal.

'Look, over there.' Joan pointed to a break in the clouds.

Sunbeams burst through the clouds like arrows shot down to the earth. Within seconds, the intense sun rays were on top of them and just as quickly, passed over, until fading into the horizon.

The winds calmed, the clouds evaporated, and the sky returned to blue. Together, the droning noise above and the wild racket of animals below faded to silence.

Mercy slumped back into her chair, unable to wipe the grin off her face.

'We call it the Solar Wave. It crosses the Shade's surface at least once a day. The noise is the result of the pressure on the surface. The wave modifies the atmosphere for each biome, ensuring they get the right amount of solar radiation and moisture required for their ecosystem,' explained the Ambassador.

'I'm speechless,' Mercy said, her heart still racing. 'I've never seen or imagined...I mean, how did you get so far ahead of us? Do you understand what this technology could do for the Sanctuary of Europe?'

The Ambassador shot a glance at Theo, a silent command to not speak.

Mercy wiped the smile from her face, feeling she had crossed some unbreachable line of diplomacy. 'I'm sorry,' she offered, hoping the damage wasn't irreparable.

'These are not matters for us, Doctor. You'll have the opportunity to discuss the future with our Prime.' Her tone distant but not scolding. 'We should continue now. She is waiting for us.'

# CHAPTER FIVE

The ship travelled deeper inland, heading for the city.

Ambassador Joan and Private Theo sat silent, allowing Mercy a private moment to soak in the spectacle of the Belt unfolding below her.

Images stored in Mercy's mind from videos and school lessons were rapidly replaced with landscapes as real as her flesh. The dense forests and overgrown grasslands were made even more otherworldly by the sheer abundance of wildlife in motion; from birds in murmuration to roaming buffalo and migrating elk to zebras and mustangs grazing to hippo, rhino and elephant bathing, to lions and hyenas stalking.

Ambassador Joan made a call to the White Tower. The voice on the other end, someone called Private Anne, confirmed their scheduled entry to the city.

Their use of first names only struck at Mercy. It seemed a counterintuitive informality for government officials.

'May I ask a personal question?' Mercy's voice tentative, anxious to avoid another breach of protocols.

'Yes, of course.' Joan's tone welcoming.

'I noticed you use your given names rather than surnames?'

Private Theo turned with eager eyes. 'We no longer use family names to identify ourselves in the Sanctuary. The Prime felt family names created division rather than unity. We are all Children of the Miracle; one family created equal.'

*Miracle? Created?* The words were cult-like. A sudden uneasiness reminded her that she knew almost nothing of the Sanctuary of Americas.

Theo went on: 'Every citizen is given a single name at birth by the Sanctuary. Even natural-children.'

Joan shot Theo a glance. Theo had given enough information.

Changing the subject, Joan announced, 'We'll be arriving at Sanctuary City in just a few moments. Our Prime is very keen to meet you, as are the other select members of government who will be in attendance. You'll need to be patient with us,' she smiled, 'none of us has had contact with anyone outside the Shade before.'

'That's something we share in common,' said Mercy, letting out a small laugh.

Ambassador Joan reached into her right pocket and produced a small metal bracelet. 'This is a PVA band. It will connect you to the virtual assistant and database we have set up for you. Please keep this on at all times during your visit. It allows you to activate most of the required facilities and communications while you're staying with us. Everyone in the Sanctuary wears one.'

Joan pulled her sleeve back, showing a similar bracelet on her wrist. Interestingly, the short hairs on the back of her hand continued up her arm.

'Once on your wrist, the assistant will personalise for you. You'll need to give it a name.'

Mercy took the bracelet without hesitation, hoping to establish a mutual sense of trust with the Ambassador. As she slipped the thin, loose metal ring over her hand, she flinched. The once-solid bracelet started shape-shifting around her wrist like a slithering snake, until it fit comfortably but snugly, incapable of slipping off on its own. Without warning, she felt a prick underneath her lower forearm where the bracelet met her flesh.

'Ouch,' she bleated and was immediately embarrassed.

'Bio imprint complete. Viral scan negative. Entry to Sanctuary City approved,' said the bracelet in a female voice. 'Hello, Doctor Mercy Perching. I'll be your assistant. How would you like to address me?'

Mercy hadn't expected a new PVA. She thought privately for a brief moment. It didn't feel right giving this one the same identifier as Gia, her lifetime companion.

'How about…Hope? I think that is something we all have in common.' She offered the Ambassador a friendly smile.

'Confirmed. Hope is now my identifier,' responded the PVA. 'I can be both voice-activated, or –' without notice, Mercy felt a tingle in her wrist bone and heard the PVA's voice inside her head, '– we can communicate via the subvocalisation method for privacy.'

Mercy never liked using bone conduction and neurotechnological communication with Gia. Her head was one of the few places she could escape, and she preferred to keep it that way.

'*Remain in voice activation until requested otherwise*', thought Mercy to her new PVA.

'Understood,' responded Hope out loud. 'I've received your itinerary for the rest of the day. Would you like to go through it?'

Ambassador Joan interrupted, 'Hope, I will cover today's itinerary with Doctor Perching. Please prepare her living quarters and alert Doctor Chase to her arrival.'

'Understood, Ambassador Joan.'

Mercy caught that Joan had overriding command of the PVA. *Useful information to keep in mind, she thought.*

'We are approaching Sanctuary City,' called out Theo.

The amber, green and gold living landscapes came to an abrupt halt, held back by an impenetrable four-hundred-foot grey concrete wall. Mercy recognised the enormous human-made structure, a mirror of the one that surrounded her own Sanctuary. But what lay beyond the city gateway confirmed how far apart the sister sanctuaries had become.

A world away from the stone and brick buildings burrowed deep into the earth for protection from solar radiation, Americas' Sanctuary City towered overhead without restrictions, both exposed and beautiful. Monolithic alloy skyscrapers shot to the heavens, dwarfing the imposing border wall. A corrugated skyline of densely stacked buildings wrapped around itself in concentric rings, layering inward and upward, always taller, until reaching the tallest building of them all: a single needle-shaped ivory tower at the heart of the city.

'The building in the centre, the White Tower, is our seat of government. That's where you'll be meeting the Prime and working while here,' explained Joan.

The ship ceased moving forward and began a smooth horizontal ascent up the wall face. Once over the summit, the flying vehicle glided into Sanctuary City.

Up close, the halo of Sanctuary City beamed brightly in the reflection of the sun. For all the god-like vision and tenacious innovation that had re-birthed a world of plants, animals and living landscapes outside the city, the world inside had discarded nature. Flying cars and artificial lights replaced the migrating herds and the forest-felt-green of the Belt. The urban sprawl of buildings old and new pushed out against the wall's edge, threatening to spill over.

'May I ask your population reclamation stats?'

'We are roughly forty million in the city. Growth is ten percent annually.'

'Astonishing. How do you feed everyone?'

'While we don't allow habitation on the Green Belt, we do use the plains and lakes for farming and fishing.'

On cue, a chain of twenty flying vehicles, ten times the size of the Ambassador's ship, steadily passed over their heads.

'Are they going into the Belt?' Mercy asked.

'Yes. The ship is likely carrying workers for the farms. They go out each day and return each evening.'

'Can anyone go into the Belt?'

'Not without government certification or a permit,' answered Ambassador Joan.

Theo spoke up: 'We also have Green Belt national holidays four times a year. Residents can go into designated areas and enjoy the natural landscapes without a permit.'

It hit Mercy that humans were no longer trusted with nature here in the Sanctuary of Americas. The Belt was sacred and protected with a sense of reverence as if it were a private chapel.

'Do you think it would be possible for me to visit the Belt?' Mercy's voice hopeful, not wanting to create another awkward situation.

'I'm sure we can arrange that,' affirmed the Ambassador.

The heart of the city was a hive of flying vehicles zipping orderly in a patchwork of invisible arteries between the condensed buildings. Private Theo joined a central, heavily used lane. The conveyer belt of vehicles was heading inward to the heart of Sanctuary City. Arriving outside the White Tower, they hovered in front of an open docking bay while a bright blue light rolled through the ship. A voice over the holodeck confirmed their approval to land.

Ambassador Joan stood, facing Mercy. 'The Prime will greet us in the docking bay. She has asked for a private meeting with you immediately after we port. Once you've finished, I'll return and escort you to the Hall of Science inside the White Tower. There you will meet Doctor Chase, who heads the government Population Research and Development Department. He has received the summary report you sent through and is looking forward to meeting you.'

The ship floated to a gentle stop inside the building. The docking bay, housing five other ships of the same size as the Ambassador's, had a military air. Metal-constructed walls and floors with rubberised walkways were illuminated by green arrows directing traffic. Guards in perfectly cut blue bodysuits, with laser guns strapped around their waists, moved about the bay and adjoining ships busy in work.

Standing at the doorway into the White Tower, under a metal sign reading MILITARY PERSONNEL ONLY, and flanked by two guards, was the Prime. Thin in frame and upright, she had one hand tucked halfway into a flat front coat pocket, and the other hung at her side. Her full lips curled slightly upwards on the ends in a guarded smile. Dark ebony skin hid her age, but the coarse silver hair tied back tight behind her head, gave away her maturity. Pinned on her chest, was a symbol of sun and flag: a circular brooch, coloured in red, white and blue metal. She stared directly at Mercy with stern but trustworthy eyes.

'Welcome, Doctor Perching.' The Prime's grin widened into a well-rehearsed smile. 'I'm Prime Orla of the Sanctuary of Americas.' Her once pocketed hand outstretched.

Mercy unconsciously straightened her back; an effort to appear more official than her weak knees might give away. She accepted the Prime's hand, noting the usual and expected bare flesh.

'Madame Prime. On behalf of the Sanctuary of Europe, we'd like to thank you for extending the invitation. While the circumstances that have brought us back together are unfortunate, we hope this is a broader opportunity to build new bridges between our nations,' recited Mercy, precisely as she had rehearsed in the mirror back home.

The Prime narrowed her eyes but continued to smile. 'Perhaps, yes, a future together. For now, though, we have a mutual goal. Let us start there.'

Mercy understood the underlying message: wait and see. Their future would depend on the outcome of the mission.

'Please, join me in my briefing room,' the Prime invited.

# CHAPTER SIX

The briefing room was on the top floor of the White Tower. Transparent ceiling to floor walls offered lighthouse views of the otherworldly city landscape below.

The open heights caught at Mercy, making her dizzy. After a few minutes, she summoned the courage to look down. The high-altitude vantage point revealed Sanctuary City to be a series of connected inner circles, each a separate sub-city of alloy skyscrapers. Layers of flying vehicles filled the air, speeding along invisible expressways, occasionally rising or dropping down lanes to change their direction. Below the busy skyways, where metal met the urban decay of stone structures, a criss-cross of glass tubed travellators ushered crowds of citizens from one building to the next.

The Prime spoke privately to Joan, who nodded and left with the two guards, leaving only Mercy in the room.

'Please have a seat, Doctor Perching,' invited the Prime, pointing to the only furniture in the room.

Four sectional sofas faced each other, forming a ring around a low table which was also a holographic generator. Small tables at the ends of each sectional hosted dishes overflowing with large and vibrantly coloured fruits – a stark contrast to the pale micro fruit grown in bio-farms underneath the Earth's world. She hoped they would be on offer.

'First, let me thank you for agreeing to come alone and without much details. I can imagine you are feeling tremendous pressure for both yourself and your Sanctuary, as well as some confusion. I'll be honest. I'm also feeling the pressure. My decision to breach the ancient agreement between our cities didn't go down well with my government. The mutation has proven to be a humbling reversal of fortune for us.'

Mercy interrupted: 'I'm sorry. Reversal of fortune?'

'We pride ourselves on our technology. We invented the Shade to protect the city from the sun. Then we learned how to harness the sun's power and to use it in safe doses to rebuild healthy ecosystems. The Shade and the Belt are probably the greatest achievements of humankind. So, the idea that we needed help – well, that was difficult for my government to swallow.'

'You mean you need help from us. A nation not quite so advanced,' answered Mercy, raising her eyebrows.

'Please don't take it as an insult. I'm happy you're here and will admit that we need help.'

'Madame Prime, one thing I don't understand. Why just me? I could have brought my entire lab team to help with your research.'

'Of course.' She paused, contemplating the right words. 'What I'm going to share with you may be difficult to understand. It may even have you question your decision to help us.'

Mercy's eyes widen with nervous anticipation. 'Please, continue.'

'Shortly after we broke off communication between the Sanctuaries, we approved a path of scientific exploration that was vehemently disapproved of by the other two Sanctuaries. Knowing that mammals had a natural resistance to the virus, we tried introducing animal DNA into living humans. But we continued to encounter insertional mutagenesis, making gene modification in living humans improbable.'

Mercy's stomach twisted on hearing her theory deflated before she had had the chance to start.

The Prime went on: 'So, we took a different route. We began modification at the cellular level. We developed a functioning hybrid foetus, part-human and part-animal, that would be immune to the virus. The new species, which in theory would be closer to human DNA, could offer a compatible gene sequence for the human genome.

'Positive results came quickly, and we continued to push all boundaries on genetic modification of interspecies fertilisation. We bent, if not outright removed, any shared ethical codes we might have had with your Sanctuary long ago.'

The Prime paused and took a declarative breath, drawing out a dramatic silence for impact. 'You'll need to prepare yourself, Doctor Perching. What you're about to experience is nothing short of a miracle. Our scientists have developed an entirely new species. We call them the Chimera.'

The hair on Mercy's neck stiffened and tiny bumps trickled up her arm. Suddenly it became clear why she had been chosen for this mission. If the Prime knew her research, she could assume Mercy would be predisposed to human genome manipulation. But the Prime's directive, breeding an entirely new species, went much further than even she had dared to imagine.

The Prime's hunch was right. Mercy was intrigued.

'Would I be able to review your research on the Chimera species while I'm here?' Mercy asked in a voice nearly pleading.

With a slight nod and a grin, the Prime continued: 'That you will, Doctor. In fact, it would be hard not to. Chimeras have moved well beyond a research project. The species are sentient, in their fourth generation, and fully integrated into our society. The first generation is now reaching thirty years of age. In total, Chimeras make up twenty percent of our population growth.'

Mercy leaned back; confusion clouded her eyes, 'Madame Prime, you're saying the Chimeras live…with humans…as equals?'

The Prime lifted one eyebrow and grinned. 'That is precisely what I'm saying. You've already met two.'

'The Ambassador?' Mercy's voice trailed off as she put the pieces of the puzzle together. *The white fur on Joan's hand.*

'Yes, and soon you will meet many more. But for now, we have to discuss the matter that has brought you to our city. Two months ago, my Chief Medical Officer announced the discovery of a new mutation of FossilFlu by our infectious disease team working on a vaccination. The new strain of the disease appears to be a mutation caused by exposure to Chimera biology.

'I've not shared this information with the public. While Chimeras live among us, some believe we have crossed a moral line and openly oppose all modification to the human genome and the Chimeras' existence. If news of a possible mutation to FossilFlu caused by exposure to Chimeras gets out, it will ignite a war here in my Sanctuary. This is the reason I have risked everything to bring you here. Our scientists are in a race against time to find a cure before the mutation happens on its own. I have some of the greatest minds working on the problem, but answers are not coming fast enough. I hope that your research and ideas will bring a fresh perspective to our own.'

Mercy's cheeks turned red, 'I'm honoured you think so highly of my work. Honestly, looking at all you have achieved, I'm not sure what I can bring to the table. But I will try to help. I owe that to my people. If this mutation spreads, your internal political battles will be the least of our problems.'

'Thank you, Doctor.' The Prime stood. 'One last request. Only a handful of Senators know about the Sanctuary of Europe and your visit. Revealing your Sanctuary's existence beyond the select few who know would cause equally devastating instability. Do you understand?'

'Of course,' Mercy replied genuinely, having heard the same from the Leaders.

'To help avoid questions, we've given you a cover. Citizens of the Americas only use given names, so as of now, Doctor, you're just Mercy, no more Perching. We've constructed an entire history and identity for you in our systems should anyone want to look you up. Ambassador Joan will walk you through the details in your private quarters after we finish here. If you keep your real identity in confidence, in return, you will be allowed to move about in public as a resident, without restriction.'

Mercy placed a hand over the thin metal bracelet around her wrist. *Without restriction but not without eyes on her at all times*, she thought. She steadied her shoulders and extended a hand, accepting the agreement. 'Madame Prime. I appreciate the trust, and I look forward to learning more about your city and all of its citizens while I'm here.'

The Prime accepted her hand. 'Good.' Before they broke away, the Prime slightly tightened her grip, locked eyes with Mercy and said, 'Doctor, I want to be clear on one point. I'm not asking for you or your government's approval about our hybrids. The Chimeras are equals among us. I will protect them at all costs, as I would protect any citizen of the Sanctuary.'

'Of course,' Mercy answered, allowing the tight grip, and slightly shaken by the maternal intensity of her defence.

The Prime called for Ambassador Joan before excusing herself, 'I'm sorry I don't have more time right now. I am sure you have a million questions. We can talk more tonight. There is a state dinner to introduce you to the Senate leaders of the Health and Security Council, who know of your visit along with

Doctor Chase, our head of Infectious Disease Research.'

'I look forward to it,' Mercy lied, large-scale diplomacy sounded awful to her.

Ambassador Joan entered the room. Mercy tried hard not to stare invasively at the hybrid. A new species, all along, right under her nose. *Unbelievable!*

If the Ambassador noticed her conspicuous behaviour, she gave no concern. *Perhaps,* Mercy thought, *because I'm the real curiosity in this place.*

# CHAPTER SEVEN

The lift opened on floor two hundred and forty-four. Joan led the way down a windowless hallway bathed in luminescent blue light.

'We'll be stopping at the Population Research and Development Centre ahead. This is where we've prepared your office next to Doctor Chase, whom you will briefly meet,' Joan announced. 'I believe his role is similar to the one you hold in your government's Reclamation Department.'

'Yes, it does sound similar,' Mercy replied distantly, distracted by the strange fluorescent light that appeared to be coming from the walls themselves. She reached out to touch the surface.

Joan smiled. 'It's bio-phosphorescent bacteria that feed off the solar radiation on the Shade.'

'What a clever idea – using binary fission to create a source of internal light. It's so simple,' Mercy pondered more to herself than her host.

Ambassador Joan stopped before a large door. To the right, a plaque read POPULATION RESEARCH AND DEVELOPMENT CENTRE. Below the sign, a digital security access panel just large enough to place a hand.

'Before we go any further, Doctor Mercy, I understand the Prime has told you about my species.'

'Yes,' replied Mercy, desperate to ask a thousand questions, but polite enough not to.

'Then I should let you know that Doctor Chase is a C10 hybrid.'

'Sorry, what's a C10?'

Suddenly realising the Prime hadn't fully briefed Mercy, the Ambassador explained: 'The goal of hybrid breeding is variation. We aim to fracture the human evolutionary path in as many different directions as we can to ensure survival. However, there are rules – guidelines for acceptable hybrid breeds so that we can live together in a productive society. There are ten hybrid classifications measured by physical attributes. A C1 is the closest line to original human DNA. A C10 is the furthest evolution from the human genome allowed. All hybrids must exhibit a human capacity for reasoning and problem solving, the ability to show empathy and to control instinct, be capable of vocal communication, be bipedal, and display compatible reproductive organs to female and male humans.'

*A god's list,* Mercy thought; the deconstruction of what makes humankind. *Who made these choices?* She wondered, *and how many mistakes did it take to get it right?*

Joan continued, 'Variances beyond those basic genetic requirements determine your classification. I'm a level C2. My DNA is human and seal's mix.' She shared this matter of factly as if describing her eye or hair colour. 'As you can see, I display primarily human characteristics. A C10 would display the most animal-like – or if you will, the least human. Any foetus classified with features above level ten is terminated.'

Mercy's shoulders shivered. As a scientist herself, she understood the need for objectivity in research. However, something of the removed nature in the way Joan talked about the culling of her own species left her cold.

Joan continued, 'The development of C1 to C8 levels is prefered, but a few C9s and C10s are allowed if they exhibit unique DNA sequencing that could help us develop better hybrids in the future. However, C9s and C10s are sterilised at birth. The risk of their offspring regressing and presenting with unsanctioned features is too high.

'Doctor Chase is a C10 from canine DNA. He will not present like any species you have ever seen before. But rest assured, he is human enough, and one of our brightest genealogists.'

Joan placed her hand on the security panel. A viridescent light beamed on, and her PVA bracelet agreed, glowing with the same green light.

'Oh, one other note,' Joan interrupted, leaning back towards Mercy with a slight smile, 'Doctor Chase can be a bit grumpy when he thinks you're staring at him. Best try not to draw attention to his appearance.'

A voice from the panel spoke: 'Access granted, Ambassador Joan.'

*Swoosh.* The metal door slid open.

Fluorescent halos of digital displays hung in clouds over rows and rows of grey cubicles lining the floor of the department of population research. Quietly, employees dressed in identical beige uniforms, sat with their faces hidden behind partitions – the low murmurs of their soft voices talking privately to their PVAs commanded silence from visitors.

At the far end of the laboratory, a tall and broad-shouldered man stood in half-shadows, his back to Mercy and Joan. He wore the same ashen uniform as the array of zealous scientists circling him, hanging on to his words like children at storytime. His thick and wavy hair stopped at his shoulders. Particular attention had been paid to brushing the coarse locks into place, holding back an otherwise unyielding dense mane of hair.

The adoring gaze of this audience slowly shifted away from him and towards Joan and Mercy. Doctor Chase turned his head. Mercy fought back a gasp. Her stomach clenched as her mind desperately tried to make sense of the creature looking directly at her. More canine than man, his appearance was neither immediately attractive nor hideous, merely impossible, familiar features in a very unfamiliar form. His profile gave the distinct impression of a hound somehow framed within a human-shaped skull. The backwards-sloping forehead ended with a soft, almost non-existent brow, allowing his round ice-blue eyes, separated slightly farther than a human's by a recessed nose bridge, to dominate the upper third of his face. His elongated jaw ended with two large front-facing nostrils made of porous black cartilage and separated by a bony septum. Skin flaps hung underneath his nose, forming an upper lip.

The creature's erect pointed ears suddenly moved in two different directions. Mercy's heart beat wildly. Her mouth hung open, gaping. The dog-man's flat eyebrows furrowed and his nostrils flared. Mercy's palms went wet. He smelled the air. She stared at him with horrified eyes. His quizzical expression shifted, darkened, took the form of a very recognisable human expression: anger. The doctor stormed determinedly towards the two visitors.

'Doctor Chase,' Joan greeted him politely, ignoring his obvious annoyance.

He pointed his eyes aggressively at her face and spoke in a harsh whisper, 'We were supposed to meet in private, Ambassador.'

Unlike a dog, his lips moved with the muscle control of a human mouth, but the exposed long sharp teeth were decidedly non-human. Swiftly, and unexpectedly, Mercy's fear suddenly turned to an insatiable curiosity as she watched the creature talk. He refused to meet her examination face to face.

Joan responded calmly, 'I'm sorry. But the Prime thought it better if Doctor Mercy get acquainted with your department as soon as possible.' Her voice dropped to a whisper. 'And we don't want to draw any particular attention. Doctor Mercy is just a visiting scientist, like any other,' said Joan, tilting her head and smiling stubbornly.

Mercy thought she heard a low growl come from the doctor before he relented to the Ambassador's unflinching stare.

Turning to Mercy, he held out a human-shaped hand. 'I'm sorry for my rudeness. Welcome Doctor Mercy; I'm Doctor Chase.'

Burnt amber fur rolled out of the sleeve of his uniform down the back of his hand. Black claws, clipped blunt and well cared for, grew in place of human fingernails. His palm: bare-skinned, dark, and padded; gripped her skinny pink fingers with gentle confidence.

There was a prolonged silence. Mercy knew it was too long. *Don't hesitate. You're a guest—a diplomat. Pull yourself together. TALK, MERCY!*

'Thank you, Doctor Chase. It's my pleasure. I've heard a lot about you,' she stumbled over the blundering choice of words and quickly tried to recover. 'Your work, that is.'

'Thank you. Can I suggest we carry on in my office?' Doctor Chase said, pointing to the doorway at the end of the room.

As the door closed to Doctor Chase's office, he motioned to a small lounge area with two sofas facing each other. 'Have a seat,' he invited them.

Mercy sat while the Ambassador remained standing near the door. Chase shrugged his shoulders in a *'suit yourself'* manner and grunted at Joan. He took a seat facing Mercy.

'Doctor Perching. Sorry for the rather informal greeting. We were originally planned to meet you when you arrived, but I'm guessing my appearance might have been the reason for our delayed introduction.' His voice caustic, his target Joan.

'We are all here now. And I believe you will agree; there are more important matters that we should be discussing.' Joan tried to calm his mood.

Mercy broke the tension as quickly as she could. 'Doctor Chase, I'm grateful for the invitation. We were deeply concerned when we heard about the FossilFlu mutation. I have to confess; your Sanctuary's technological achievements have somewhat humbled me since arriving. I can only hope you will find my research useful.'

Chase let out a brief relinquishing grunt. 'I'm sure we both have a lot to learn from each other. Your briefing notes were impressive. Thank you for sending those in advance. While we've managed to engineer an entirely new species – well, several species – to combat FossilFlu extinction, we still hadn't uncovered the source of immunity in mammals. And now...' he trailed off in thought but quickly recovered, '...now we have an even bigger problem to solve.' The simple statement sounded sincere and regretful. 'I have set up your lab next to my office. Your PVA...' he paused, waiting for Mercy to clarify.

'Hope,' she volunteered.

'Hope will be given access to our research on the mutation.'

'Excuse me, Doctor Chase, but may I also request access to your work regarding Chimeras?'

Chase pinched his brow tightly, a look that bordered on furiousness. Mercy quickly glanced to Joan, looking for validation, worried that the use of the word Chimera might have offended Chase.

'It's just that it would help me understand the new strain,' she continued apologetically, 'if I also understand the host environment that allowed it to mutate.'

Chase rolled his eyes over to Joan.

'The Prime said *all research*,' Joan volunteered.

Chase gave a defeated shake of his head and a grunt. 'Of course,' he continued in a tone that was almost a threat. 'My only request is that you remember this is still my lab, and there are rules.'

Something snapped in Mercy. Dog or man, she wasn't one to be told what to do in a lab. 'Doctor Chase, I completely respect that this is your department, and of course, I will work within your protocols. However, I didn't leave my home, fly halfway around the planet, and enter a possible contagious zone, to be your employee. I suggest we approach this opportunity as one to work together. You and I. Equals.'

Joan smiled. Mercy held his stare.

Chase sat back, releasing a sigh and a grunt of conciliation. 'Of course. I didn't mean to insinuate otherwise. Tomorrow we'll start by meeting the team working on the mutation. I'm sure the Prime has shared that this information remains highly confidential. Only a select few of my best have clearance. Discussing research on the mutation outside of this group is forbidden.'

'Yes, I understand. The Prime informed me of the political consequences at stake.'

Chase, unable to hide his emotions behind his overtly expressive eyebrows, became angry again but said nothing.

Joan interrupted, 'Good. Glad we are all agreed on the next steps. I'll show Doctor Mercy to her quarters now. You two will have more time to catch up tonight at the state dinner.'

As they left Chase's office, slowly, very slowly, Mercy's mind was starting to adjust, and the dog was becoming a man.

# CHAPTER EIGHT

The door to the State Room slid open. All eyes were on Mercy as she entered. Her wardrobe had been provided: a floor-length white tunic with tails and trousers belted with an ebony-coloured sash. She was in a very grand room, bright and warm; for a golden sunset bled in through invisible walls. Mercy got the impression of floating over the city.

Six Senators, four in white tunics and two in all black, were sprinkled around the room. The dark clothed Senators, noticeably separated from the others, kept to themselves.

The Prime, having just cut off her conversation with Doctor Chase, smiled at Mercy and Ambassador Joan. Spreading her arms wide, she drew them to her side.

'May I have everyone's attention, please,' she broadcast, waving her hands inward, a command for all to join her.

The Senators in white hurried around her expectantly. The Senators in black joined less enthusiastically.

Mercy's attention was on one Senator in particular – a Chimera who bore the markings of a cat. Her large, round, emerald eyes and a flat upturned black nose, more button than snout, were framed in pink flesh. The feline-woman had long coarse whiskers that sprung up to her cheeks where a human would have a moustache. Her calico hairline formed a heart with a peak low on her forehead, curving back around her human-shaped ears and under her lower jowl.

*How random,* Mercy thought. Having had a few hours alone in her quarters to digest Chase's appearance hadn't helped reduce the surprise of seeing another C10 in the flesh. The hybrid features of the feline's body, while recognisable and oddly natural, continued to strike Mercy as fictitious, like a storybook character.

The Prime continued her address: 'Senators, I'd like to take this opportunity to introduce Doctor Mercy.' She turned to address Mercy directly: 'Doctor, myself, and the Senators would like to welcome you to the Sanctuary of Americas.'

The Prime went down the line of Senators offering personal introductions. Mercy received smiles and nods from most. Except for the Senator from District one known as Arjun, who stood with arms crossed and a pinched pale face. His black tunic draped off his bony shoulders like a cloak on a hanger. His black beady eyes were in a constant state of suspicion, and his thin lips curled permanently downward. An ink-black braid hung low down his back. As the Prime called his name, he greeted Mercy with a half-nod. The Prime moved on quickly, dismissing his belligerence.

'I'd like to thank everyone for joining me tonight,' the Prime continued in a sombre tone. 'We are here because we face a potential crisis worse than anything we've seen before. Even the slightest risk of another FossilFlu epidemic requires that we focus all our resources on developing a vaccine. And such is the urgency that we must consider unconventional steps and act decisively.'

The Senators listened in silence.

'I know not everyone agreed with my decision to contact the Sanctuary of Europe. It is true, in the past, distrust clouded our relationship with our once sister city. But long before that, we worked together, successfully, to stop the spread of FossilFlu and save humanity. I believe we can find that trust and faith again. Together we will be stronger, wiser and better prepared.'

Nods of confirmation came from the four Senators in white.

The Prime went on: 'Now, the Sanctuary of Europe could have refused or challenged our conditions. Instead, they openly accepted our invitation on all our terms and sent us their brightest scientific leader without question. If we don't show the same trust by opening up our city and our science to Doctor Mercy, then what kind of a society are we?'

Senator Arjun squinted his eyes and frowned sourly, knowing he was the target of her comment.

'I say our future,' the Prime continued raising a hand to Mercy and Chase, 'all our futures, human and Chimera alike, are safer today thanks to Doctor

Mercy and Doctor Chase.'

Mercy nodded her agreement and thank you at once. Chase stood with arms tucked behind his back, eyes cast to the ground, and gave a nod of his head, humbly accepting her praise.

'Now, please, let us dine and welcome Doctor Mercy after her long journey,' concluded the Prime, waving everyone to the table.

Mercy sat between the Prime on her left and Doctor Chase on her right. The table was dressed as if for a celebration: white starch linens, gold cutlery and porcelain plates. Ten waiters appeared carrying glass bottles and having white linen napkin draped over their forearms. Synchronised, they filled the tall skinny flutes at the head of each plate. An effervescent gold liquid gurgled into the clear glasses, giving rise to an endless fountain of tiny bubbles coalescing into a foaming head.

As the waiters finished in perfect simultaneity, Chase plucked his drink from the table. Leaning towards Mercy, he said, 'We don't get this every day, Doctor Mercy.'

'What is it?' She asked, rather coyly.

Chase shot her a dumbfounded stare. 'Champagne,' he blurted out with some astonishment. 'Made from California vines kept in the food archives during the days of rationing.'

'Oh, yes, I've heard about California, the state that sank below the rising ocean. We have a children's story that tells of the great city of San Francisco. Superior in technology and wealth to all others. Some even claim the city is still secretly thriving, under the ocean, safe from the sun.'

Chase burst out laughing, 'What, like the mythical city of Atlantis?'

Mercy blushed, suddenly embarrassed. 'I guess, yes, it's just a children's story after all.'

Chase erased his smile immediately, not wanting to embarrass her further. 'I can assure you, nothing of the State of California exists anymore, above or below the ocean. Except for these vines. Enjoy it; this is one of the perks of a dinner with the Prime,' he smiled, sending his glass into hers for a clinking cheer.

Mercy held the drink to her nose. It smelled nuttily sweet. She took a sip. Bubbles suddenly shot up the back of her throat, into her nose, as she coughed. The Senators looked at her quizzically and with humour. She felt compelled to explain.

'I'm sorry; we don't have champagne in our Sanctuary. Food production is limited to essentials only,' she confessed.

Her candid disclosure granted the Senators the permission they sought to intrude further. Like vultures to a fresh carcass, they rushed at her with their questions about the Sanctuary of Europe, politely asked and Mercy always answered.

*The population of the Sanctuary of Europe was just under twelve million.*
*Most of the citizens lived and worked below the Earth's surface.*
*Water and food were heavily rationed but readily available.*
*Their supply of water came from desalinisation of the salt lakes and by recycling.*
*Food was grown in underground farms and biospheres on the Earth's surface.*
*Their energy source was solar, but the desert dust caused significant problems.*

Time passed and the questions slowed. Waiters continued to arrive with seasonal foods beautifully laid out to showcase the artistry of the chef. Painted streaks of beet-red and mint-green puree splashed across white china dishes, mounted with meticulously cut, cooked and positioned vegetables, grains and fruits. Each plate a new design, the next always superseding the previous in bold and delicate presentations.

Some of the foods Mercy recognised, but many she had only read about from before the Scorch. After the embarrassment of the champagne incident, she held back her insatiable curiosity. *What were the names of the plants, where did they grow, and under what conditions?* She would have asked.

Throughout the dinner, Senator Arjun remained suspiciously quiet, devoid of questions – fork and knife clipping his plate, listening while stuffing the night's feast into his mouth.

As the waiters brought out the last meal, chocolate mousse and cherry crisp, when the conversations had slowed, Arjun took his long-awaited opportunity.

'Doctor Perching,' he called out, silencing the room by punctuating his use of her surname. 'I believe we can respectfully call you by your full name in this private environment.'

Mercy, lightheaded from all the food and champagne, missed his critical intent and answered him innocently, 'No, that's fine. I'm happy to use Mercy while here.'

The irked Senator's mouth tightened. He continued, 'Very well, then, diplomacy it is. I'm curious – what do you think your people will make of our beloved Chimeras?'

Chase slammed his silverware on his plate, broadcasting his contempt. The feline-woman, whom Mercy had come to know as Senator Jasper, mirrored Chase's shock. The emerald green of her eyes nearly swallowed by a rapidly expanded black pupil. Her upper lip curled and quivered, showing off her thin, razor-like teeth.

'You don't have to answer that, Doctor,' the Prime quickly interrupted.

Senator Arjun persisted belligerently, angered by the Prime's intervention. 'Please, Prime, with all respect, I have sat here for several hours listening to idle chit-chat as if this were nothing more than a cultural exchange! Now I ask for just a few moments, and then I will dismiss myself.'

The Prime met his hardened stare with an eye that commanded he be careful, and then, with a graceful nod, gave her approval for him to continue.

'Doctor Mercy, you should be aware that not everyone here agrees with the genetic mutations we call Chimeras.'

Chase let out a low growl.

'They did not evolve over thousands of years, cultivated by nature to fit into the world around them,' continued Arjun, unabashed. 'We still have no idea how these new species will impact our world and ecosystems. And now, proving my point, breeding human with an animal was not the saviour we were promised. Instead, it has given us the deadliest virus known to humankind. We may have just killed every living animal on this planet. This is what we should be talking about tonight. The real cause of our *crisis.*' He pointed his eyes daringly at Chase.

'That's enough, Senator!' commanded the Prime. 'Let me remind everyone at this table that our purpose together is shared. Our hope is shared. To find a cure, not just for humans, but for everyone.'

'Hear! Hear!' cheered the Senators in white.

Slamming his fist on the table, Arjun stood and stormed out of the room, followed sheepishly by the other Senator in black. Chase, red-faced with rage, sounded off a low, threatening growl after him.

A profound silence sat in the room. No one spoke before the Prime.

'Doctor Mercy, accept my apologies. Senator Arjun was out of line. He and Senator Agnis' views are not representative of the vast majority of citizens of the Sanctuary. Regardless, this is not the place for him to make his case. The Chimeras are citizens of the Sanctuary like all others, and we don't tolerate hate rhetoric.' The Prime raised her glass, 'Doctor Chase and Doctor Mercy, we are in your hands. Be swift.'

Everyone drank.

Ambassador Joan escorted Mercy back to her chambers.

'What happened in there?' Mercy's question hesitant, not wanting to push Joan into an uncomfortable conversation.

Joan pondered a response. 'Senator Arjun belongs to the Purist Party, as do most of his constituents in District One, which is primarily human.

'They have fought the science of hybrids since the beginning, believing only in natural evolution. They argue that human intervention with nature created global warming and the virus. The new strain of FossilFlu has emboldened their cause. They hope not only to end the disease but hybrids as well.'

'You mean end hybrid breeding, not the living Chimeras. Right?'

'Let's leave it there, shall we? I imagine you would like some time to recuperate before your meeting tomorrow morning,' Joan smiled, arriving at Mercy's apartment door. She said her goodbyes.

Back in her apartment, Mercy stood before the ceiling-to-floor glass wall facing the Belt.

'Hope?' Mercy called into the air.

'Yes, Doctor?'

'Are there windows in this apartment?'

'Certainly, Doctor.'

To Mercy's amazement, directly in front of her, the wall rippled liquid, and the transparent material slithered outward to form a long horizontal opening. Suddenly it was as though the air had come alive. A brisk, fresh evening wind blew at Mercy. She inhaled long and deep and stretched her hands over her head. What a strange and curious world the Sanctuary of Americas turned out to be, she thought.

# CHAPTER NINE

The meeting room in the Department of Population Research and Development was dimly lit. The holographic display at the centre of a large oval conference table read *MUTATION FFv1, Highly Classified*. Twelve scientists sat in the round, paused in waiting; their eager faces turned pallid by the glow of the virtual presentation. Almost all were Chimera. Their large eyes, upturned snouts, downturned ears, hair, fur, wool and whiskers, were on full display.

'Good morning, everyone,' Chase called out from the top of the table, Mercy standing by his side. 'I'd like to introduce Doctor Mercy to our project. She's an old colleague of mine who has been working in the remote regions of the Belt for many years with the Ecosystem Reclamation Unit studying animal resistance to FossilFlu. I want you to treat her as you would me, your senior. She's here for a short time to help us crack the code on Mutation FFv1 so we can get on with a possible vaccination.'

Curious eyes met Mercy's. She took a seat next to Chase who pointed to a young man with ribbed horns curling from the top of his skull down around his distinctly human ears.

'Coby, you're up. Let's get her up to speed,' barked Chase.

The goat-boy's thin letterbox irises expanded at hearing his name called out. He drew his hand across the hologram and started scrolling through data and 3D replications of DNA.

Blinking frequently, he began: 'The FFv1 mutation acts like a bacteriophage; it can move around undetected in the genome...'

The young scientist continued for over an hour, explaining the known details of the mutation. Mercy slipped comfortably into the day, talking disease and cures. As the young Chimeras, one by one presented their work, their less than human features faded from her mind's eye. They had become just another room of scientist, like the many she had worked with before.

'I may be able to shed some light here,' Mercy would eventually interrupt. 'May I?' she asked, leaning into the hologram.

'Please,' replied a rabbit-woman, who's turn had come to an end, eager to hand over the spotlight.

Mercy commanded Hope to bring up her presentation in the holographic sphere. Years of research, many guesses proved wrong and assumptions found to be right, scrolled through the air. Her life's work summarised and divulged to hungry minds. The bewitched scientists listened with rapt attention, absorbing each note of her discoveries.

Hours passed as the day turned to night. Questions led to new and more complex problems. Problems led to hypotheses. Hypotheses led to projects. And the work ahead of them solidified.

Chase remained on the sidelines, a quiet but commanding listener. Occasionally he would throw out a question to Mercy's comment, or a correction to one of the scientists' theories. But overall Mercy took charge of the room and fell naturally into the leadership role.

Chase called the day over around ten pm. Mercy waved her hand, and in a blink, the presentation disappeared. The lights in the room came up, revealing hollow-eyed, fatigued scholars, drunk with information.

'Thank you, everyone,' said Mercy, 'for such an open welcome and sharing your research. I'm honoured to be working on this project with you and only hope I can be of assistance. I'll have my PVA upload my research into the data bank. Everyone will have access to it. And I'll see you tomorrow.'

Spontaneous applause broke out. Mercy's ivory flesh burned red.

With a grunt, Chase ended the tribute, 'Okay, okay. You're embarrassing Doctor Mercy.' He verbally ushered the troops out of the room. 'It's been a good day. We've got our marching orders. Let's get on these tests tomorrow. Have a good night, everyone.'

The scientists filed out slowly, each taking their opportunity to thank Doctor Mercy. A silver-skinned young woman, who had sat quietly during the day studiously listening and taking notes, now approached Mercy. Her large black convex eyes, protruding from opposite sides of her narrow face, moved independently, one landing vivaciously on Mercy, the other fixed on her colleagues leaving the room. The sight of it left Mercy confused, wondering which eye to follow.

Aligning both eyeballs forward, the young woman tilted her head back and stared at Mercy down her broad nose. 'Doctor Mercy, thank you for sharing your research. May I ask a question?'

'Yes,' Mercy answered, trying desperately not to stare incredulously at the human-dolphin hybrid.

'Finding the dormant immunity genes in humans is ground-breaking. I'm surprised this is the first we have heard of it. Why is that?'

The question arrested Mercy and pushed her back into the awkward political landscape of this new world. She had to think quickly.

'I'm sorry, I don't know the answer to that other than that this is a very recent discovery. I guess that's why I'm here now rather than back in the Belt,' she said with a polite smile.

'I see. That makes sense,' the dolphin-woman nodded. Her left eye wandered again as if thinking privately, solemn. The obvious uncomfortable truth sat between them. Cure humans and do away with the need for hybrids.

'But it's irrelevant now,' Mercy jumped in, determined to put the woman's fears to rest. 'The mutated strain has found a way around the virus induced resistance gene. Our work today is about a vaccine for humans and Chimeras.'

The grey-skinned woman's thick, rubber-like lips curled into a smile. 'Of course. Thank you, Doctor Mercy.' The right eye took the lead from her left as she walked out the door.

Chase sat at the table bent over a screen held in one palm, scratching notes with the other hand, his pointed ears turned forward, deep in concentration.

Mercy thought of interrupting him but suddenly felt an intruder. As the last scientist left, she turned to follow.

'Would you like to join me for a nightcap?' he asked her without looking up.

She hesitated, unsure he was addressing her directly.

Chase rolled his eyes up, surprised by the lack of an immediate answer. 'I'm sorry. Do you have other plans? I just assumed you were free.'

'No....' A flustered answer. 'I mean, yes, I'm free; no, I don't have other plans. But it's rather late?'

'Up to you. I understand if you want to call it a night. Great work today.'

He followed with an approving grunt and nod.

'Thanks. You have a strong team. They seem to work well together.'

'Young, I know, but the best minds in the Sanctuary.'

'Yes.' Mercy left the word hanging.

'I'm sorry, yes, they are the best minds or yes, you'll have a nightcap?' Chase let out a rare smirk.

'Yes, to both,' Mercy smiled back. 'I'm still rather energised from today if I'm honest. I could use a wind-down.'

'Great,' he replied, dropping his head back down and continuing note-taking while talking. 'The Prime has given us access to her private dining quarters. Hope can give you directions. I'll send Joan a note, and we can all meet in fifteen minutes.'

'Of course, yes. See you then.' Mercy left the room feeling dismissed.

# CHAPTER TEN

'Floor three hundred and seventy-seven,' announced the elevator. With a *swoosh*, the doors opened.

Two guards stood at the end of a short hallway before a closed door. One, a stout man, human in features except for the thick golden lion's mane circling his head from cheek to cheek, motioned towards the door. 'Doctor Mercy, welcome. Right this way.'

'Will the Prime be joining us tonight?' Mercy suddenly asked, worried for not having considered it before.

'No, ma'am. The Prime is not in residence. Doctor Chase and Ambassador Joan are waiting for you.'

Designed for the Prime to entertain smaller groups, the corner suite housed both a dining table and a lounge area. A long bar stretched across the back wall where rows of unlabelled glass bottles filled with coloured liquids were lined neatly on shelves.

'Doctor Mercy, please join us,' invited Joan from her seat at the bar.

Something was different about her. It wasn't just that her snow-white hair, kept tightly back on her head during the day, now tumbled down past her broad shoulders. No, something more fundamental. *Her eyes are different*, Mercy realised. Yesterday, they were human eyes, white crown around a brown iris. Now the entirety of the eye was dark brown; like a seal.

Caught staring, Mercy stumbled over her response. 'Thank – you.'

The Ambassador immediately understood. 'Sorry for the disguise yesterday. The Prime felt it would be best until she explained about hybrids.'

'I prefer them this way,' replied Mercy, quick to put the blunder behind her, and took a seat at the bar.

Hope spoke from thin air. 'What would you like to drink, Doctor Mercy?'

'Alcohol is rare in our city,' Mercy shared with Chase and Joan. 'Would you recommend something?'

Chase raised his glass. 'This is a gin and tonic. Joan has red wine.'

'Gin. I think I've read about that. Fermented agricultural produce, right?'

Hope answered before Chase could. 'Yes. The dry Gin served here is made from wheat.'

'Well, that sounds like something I should try. I'll have a gin – and – tonic,' Mercy requested.

'Good choice,' Chase confirmed, taking a long sip of his drink.

'How was your first day in the lab?' asked Joan in a friendly tone.

'Enlightening,' Mercy answered. 'Doctor Chase has been very welcoming.'

Chase offered a gracious nod in return.

Joan continued, 'Chase does not often offer praise, but he talked very enthusiastically about your presentation today.'

Chase made an affable growl; his cheeks flushed red.

'Thank you. But I'm equally impressed with the team and their work. Unravelling the mutations genome in such a short time is a remarkable result,' said Mercy.

The Gin and tonic arrived via a drone. Mercy lifted her glass. 'Cheers,' she offered.

The clanking of glasses rang, and the trio settled back into a natural conversation. Chase and Mercy discussed next steps and a few new ideas Mercy wanted to run by the team. Joan asked pointed questions and contributed to the discussion with equal measure.

'Ambassador, your knowledge of genetics is impressive.' Mercy complimented, sounding surprised.

Joan shot Chase a look as if to command him to stay quiet before answering: 'Yes. All Chimeras complete a program of genetics and molecular biosciences. We are required before the age of fifteen to have completed programs in biochemistry, structural biology, cell and development biology, and genetics and genomics.'

'All of you?' Mercy pried further, sounding even more surprised.

Chase, no longer able to remain quiet, spoke, 'You see, Doctor Mercy, we were not just designed to have DNA for study, we were also designed to study DNA.' His eyebrows raised and he smiled slyly, drawing out the sarcasm of his comment. 'We are an army of genetic scientists built to dissect ourselves and save our creators. It's the reason we were engineered to be sentient so that we can study. Otherwise, I'd likely be sitting on the floor panting at your feet right now, waiting to be patted.'

'That's why there are so many Chimeras working in your lab?' She replied, quick to ignore the uncomfortable reference to a house pet.

'Yes, and still the best minds for it,' he defended more than answered. 'It's easier for Low-Cs to stay in the program than face the racism and fear out there in public.'

'I see,' Mercy answered quietly, trying to sound respectful. 'Low-C?' she asked after a moment.

Joan answered. 'That's the street name for our classifications. High-Cs are the most human-like; Low-C displays more animal features. They are derogatory terms used by humans. Mostly behind closed doors.'

'Ambassador, you're not working in a lab, then?'

'Ten years ago, when the Prime took office, she freed the Chimera from the lab, giving us citizenship status and allowing us to choose our path. I, like many Chimera, signed up for military training shortly after. We were used to a disciplined lifestyle, and to be honest, outside of Government work, we didn't have many options in the beginning.'

*Freed*. The word sent chills down Mercy's spine. An entire species engineered to be slaves sounded barbaric.

Anxious to change the subject, Mercy asked, 'So, you and Doctor Chase know each other from before work?'

'Yes, we were in the same Generation.'

Joan peeled back her sleeve and brushed her left fingertips over the underside of her right forearm. The number G5.34.21 glowed beneath the soft white fur on the surface of her skin. Chase repeated the movement on his right forearm, revealing his id: G5.435.662.

'Is the Prime…?' Mercy asked, trailing off before saying the word Chimera out loud.

Chase laughed, 'No, she's pure. Chimeras are her family legacy. Her father served as Prime for thirty years before she took the seat. And before that, he was in charge of Population Reclamation. Hybridisation was his idea and program. I guess you could say we share the same father,' he jested.

The Prime's maternal defence of the Chimeras suddenly made sense. Mercy wanted to ask more but dared not. She worried she had reached the limit of their tolerance for her personal questions. Placing her glass on the counter to signal an exit, she said, 'I should be getting back to my quarters. Tomorrow's another long day. Thank you, both. I'm still a bit overwhelmed by all of this. Your openness about your history…maybe I shouldn't have pried.'

'Doctor Mercy, you are our guest,' Joan offered earnestly. 'We have nothing to hide. I would only suggest you don't allow yourself to get distracted by our politics. The cure is all that matters. It will not only stop a pandemic but possibly stop a war against the Chimera.'

Chase grunted and nodded in agreement. Their unspoken agenda was clear. Mercy was being recruited. Neutral was not an option: help find the cure, and she would also help the Chimera.


Sudden exhaustion weighted Mercy as she stepped off the elevator. Anxious to get back to her quarters and still heavy in thought, she hadn't noticed the hooded stranger approaching from the other direction, until, with a hard thump, they bumped into each other. Something fell onto the floor, hitting Mercy's foot.

'I'm sorry,' Mercy blurted out, startled.

The stranger, head hung low to hide his face behind the hood of its cape, spoke quietly and rushed, 'Please take it, Doctor Mercy. You're in danger.'

Her body went rigid, and her mind numb. Questions spilt out without much thought. 'Excuse me? Who are you? How do you know my name?'

The mysterious messenger spun around and quickly dashed down the hall in the direction of his arrival, turned the corner and disappeared out of sight. Mercy stared at the empty corridor wide-eyed and baffled.

Slowly, her brain started working again as she tried to make sense of the situation. *Did he say I'm in danger?* Her gaze fell to the ground where a small black object lay, accidentally dropped or intentionally left. Quickly, she collected the chip and hurried into her apartment.

Safely inside, heart still pounding, she stared at the small metal object lying on the table before her. She assumed it to be some kind of data storage.

*Why me? What kind of danger? From whom?* She asked herself nervously.

'Hope, contact Ambassador Joan,' Mercy requested immediately, then thought twice, 'Wait. Hope, cancel the call.'

Trying to calm her breath, she approached the situation logically. Who might have a reason to harm her? The Prime brought her over, so it seemed unlikely she would want to put Mercy in danger. Joan and Chase had revealed their reasons for needing Mercy's help. Senator Arjun seemed a likely candidate, blaming the Chimeras for the virus mutation. But why her? Getting rid of Mercy wouldn't stop the research.

For the first time since arriving at the Sanctuary of Americas, she truly felt alone, with no one to confide in or trust. After much deliberation, she decided to wait until the morning when she would be back in the lab and could access the secure lab PVA.


Mercy lay on her bed, unable to sleep, her mind tense. A cool breeze from an open window near her bed floated towards her. After long minutes of tossing, her worried mind, at last, gave in. She dreamed.

*Rolling dark clouds, heavy with thunder and rain swirled above her, threatening a severe storm. Winds picked up, and Mercy felt her body lighten. Desperately grappling at the ground, she couldn't stop herself from being sucked up into the violent air. With nothing to grab onto, she was tossed and twisted; lost. That's when she heard the song. A light tune was playing on a breeze. Gentle for all the ferocity surrounding her. Was it a child singing? No. A bird's song? The haunting melody, indistinguishable as human or animal, brought the storm to rest and Mercy back safely down to Earth.*

As soon as her feet landed, she bolted up in her bed wide awake, realising the song was real. And it was coming from a creature hovering outside her window looking directly at her!

Feminine in form, the young bird-girl had a short yellow toothless beak for a jaw but on a human skull with human-shaped eyes. Two large wings mounted on her back flapped rapidly like a hummingbird, keeping her frozen in space. She wore a loose sleeveless dress revealing scarlet and turquoise feathers lining her arms and neck. Her dark auburn hair, human, floated in the air on the wind of her wings. Dangling at the end of her exposed human feet were long nails sharp enough to capture, kill and carry prey.

The creature suddenly stopped singing.

'Hello?' called Mercy, not knowing what else to do.

The child-like Chimera responded with a melodic whistle, not the song that had woken Mercy from the dream, but equally pleasant and friendly.

Mercy's guard lowered. 'What do you need?'

*Whoosh.* A sudden wind blew directly at Mercy as the bird-girl's wings stretched wide, fluttering slowly at first, then faster, lighter, lifting her back away from the window.

'Wait!' Mercy begged as the creature disappeared into the night sky.

# CHAPTER ELEVEN

All seemed usual in the Department of Population Research and Development when Mercy entered. Up and down the vast laboratory, doctors and scientists sat studiously before streams of data and holographic projections; decoding, encoding and virtually splicing their way to a better version of themselves, blissfully unaware of the new viral threat.

Mercy hurried down the lab corridor, avoiding eye contact. Placing a hand on the security panel, she looked back over her shoulder nervously. The screen and her bracelet glowed green. Through the secured entrance where only those with high-level clearance were allowed, Mercy nervously dashed past Chase's office. The room was empty. Relieved, she hurried into the office set up for her and closed the door.

Pulling out the chip, she directed Hope to activate the lab PVA. A beam of light shot up from the centre of her desk.

'Hope, create and time stamp a personal log. This report is for my records, not for publishing.'

'Complete and ready for recording,' Hope confirmed.

Mercy nervously placed the chip in the holographic beam. 'Read chip,' she directed the lab PVA. Nanoseconds later, reams of ghostly data rolled down the virtual column. Mercy's eyes rapidly shifted left to right as she dissected and consumed the information, hunting for something – anything – unusual.

'It's just research on Mutation FFv1 antibody tests. The goat-boy already touched on this yesterday,' she thought out loud. *There is nothing new here. Why did he give this to me? What does it have to do with being in danger?*

A sudden noise from behind the door startled her.

'Close report,' Mercy whispered urgently, grabbing the chip and slipping it into her pocket at the exact moment Chase opened the door.

'Excuse me. I didn't know you were in here,' he said apologetically.

'Yes, sorry, I thought I would get an early start this morning. I had a few ideas last night.'

'I know the feeling,' he continued, unaware of anything out of the usual. 'Listen, Doctor Mercy…'

'Please call me Mercy,' she interrupted, hoping the personal invitation would deflect more serious questions about her morning activities.

'Very well, if you agree to call me Chase,' he smiled.

Mercy nodded.

'Listen about last night. I want you to know I understand how strange and overwhelming all this must be. The Ambassador explained that you weren't briefed on hybrids until you arrived. Just before you met me.'

'Yes, but that's no excuse. I wasn't thinking about you as a…' she stopped herself short.

'What? You didn't think of me as a person?' he finished her thought.

Mercy stumbled through an apology. 'Well, yes. But I didn't mean it that way,' she countered, sounding frustrated. 'I meant, I was only thinking of you as a scientist, instead of your feelings as a person.' Her face bled bright red.

'Please, Mercy, it's expected,' he continued with some disdain. 'Every new variant hybrid has a barrier of acceptance. Some adjust easily. Most Low-Cs, like me, are only ever tolerated. Even among other Chimeras.'

'Unfortunately, that trait sounds all too human,' Mercy acknowledged. 'You and I are not that different, Chase. I was conceived in a lab, carried by a surrogate and then raised in a government program. There are thousands like me back home. You and I, we are both parts of the next chapter in the human race. And we've both dedicated our lives to helping humankind in all its new possible forms be the best it can be.'

'I hear you,' Chase sighed sincerely. 'Shall we start again?'

'Yes,' she replied, thankful.

'I've scheduled you on a tour of the reprogramming and fertilisation facilities this morning. I hope that's alright. It will help with your Chimera research.'

'Thank you. I'd like that.'

Chase continued, 'I also understand from Joan that you'd like to visit the Belt?'

'Please, that would be incredible,' replied Mercy with excitement.

'Good. I've cleared my morning schedules today and tomorrow. I'll be your guide through the facilities this morning. And if you don't mind, the Ambassador asked me to join your first excursion to the Belt tomorrow morning. The Belt is a bit of a hobby of mine.'

Muddled feelings of flattery and susceptibility to his new charm left her wanting to get to know him better. Yet, she still felt obligated to relieve him of any duty he might be feeling to watch over her.

'Thank you, but I know you must be extremely busy. I don't want to be a burden.'

'No, no. My pleasure. Best from the horse's mouth, they say....' Chase paused with a cheeky twinkle in his eyes, 'Or, in this case, the dog's.'

Mercy grinned slightly apprehensively, unsure if his comment was playful or this was another sarcastic jab.

'I'll come to pick you up in about an hour. I've got some work to clear through this morning. I authorised your access to all research on Mutation FFv1. Enjoy.' Chase threw a hand into the air, waving goodbye, and turned to leave before she could thank him.

An idea had come to Mercy while talking with Chase. *What if the data on the chip wasn't the full report?*

Once alone, Mercy requested the lab PVA to identify the author of the research. The response came back negative. The file had no indicated source or author. Unwilling to give up easily, she took a long shot and ordered the lab PVA to filter through all research on the new virus strain, looking for a match to the report on the disk.

Fifty minutes passed when the Lab PVA announced, 'Doctor Mercy, I believe this is the full report you have requested.'

The title MUTATION FFv1 ANTI-SPARG3 materialised in the light shaft, and the conclusion, FAILED.

'Well, let's see what's hiding in this file,' Mercy said out loud. 'Hope, send a full report to my files,' she ordered. *I'll look through this after the tour.*

Just as she closed the holographic display, Chase knocked at her door.

# CHAPTER TWELVE

On floor minus twenty-one of the White Tower, over a heavily secured door, the words FERTILISATION AND INCUBATION CENTRE were etched onto a metal sign.

*Shwoop* – the hermetically sealed doorway automatically opened on Doctor Chase's command. Inside was a second chamber with another sealed door. Packets containing a pale lavender liquid lined the shelf immediately to the left. A sign on a plaque read PLEASE WASH MOUTH THOROUGHLY AND SPIT IN SINK. Mercy followed Chase's lead, unzipped a bag and delivered its contents into her mouth without question. *Whoosh* – the powerful vacuum sucked down their spit as fast as it hit the sink.

'Please place safety goggles over your eyes and step into the Antiseptic Chamber, keeping your mouths closed,' the room PVA instructed.

Goggles on, Mercy stepped into the double-glazed glass cube. A smoky iodine-based vapour filled the chamber, obscuring her vision. Seconds later, small portholes at the bottom sucked the gas back out. Stepping through to the other side of the glass cube, they found a bin full of sealed paper-like slippers and pale flesh-coloured rubber gloves. Mercy and Chase removed their shoes and goggles and slipped on the sleeves.

*Shwoop* – the second hermetically sealed door opened to the Materials Room. Cold air rushed out. Inside, placards hanging over the containers displayed the names of mammals whose cells were stored inside: *Loxodonta Africana, Pan troglodytes, Syncerus caffer, Felis concolor Linnaeus, Sylvilagus.* On and on the names of animals stretched far to the left and right. Chase walked briskly ahead of her with disinterest in the room itself. Its contents being self-explanatory.

'Do you only use mammalian DNA?' Mercy called out, hoping Chase would slow down.

'Yes, only mammalian,' he responded plainly; the obviousness of the answer required no further explanation.

Chase's certainty confused Mercy. If they only used mammal genes for hybrids, what was the bird-human who had visited her in the night?

As they neared the end of the storage room, Mercy noticed that the last twenty rows, some one hundred canisters deep each, were dedicated to a single species: *Homo sapiens*.

'Variant donors?' Mercy questioned.

'Yes. Cell donation is required by law, ensuring there is a diverse supply of human DNA. It was also felt hybrids would be more acceptable to humans if Chimeras were considered descendants of the broader population.'

'How do you avoid inbreeding?' asked Mercy.

'Labels. Our DNA mix is coded into the ID we have tattooed under our skin. Of course, neither humans nor Chimeras have direct access to the data bank for privacy reasons. PVAs are allowed access to the information and can validate an incompatibility risk before mating.'

'That must be a real mood killer,' joked Mercy.

Chase simply grunted, leaving her attempt at friendly banter lying flat on the floor.

*Shwoop* – the next door on their tour opened to the Fertilisation Room. Warm bright lights bled through the doorway, consuming the pale light of the storage chamber. Inside, the temperature rose significantly. White robot arms precisely manipulating metal syringes over glass Petri dishes spliced, edited, and reprogrammed the building blocks of life. A constant whirr of moving mechanical parts ushered the dishes filled with fertilised embryos down a conveyor belt through a small opening into the next room.

'This is where we construct hybrid embryos through interspecies somatic cell nuclear transfer using reprogrammed oocytes of varied species' cells. Coding instructions come directly from the scientists up in my lab,' Chase explained as they walked along the belt.

'Amazing,' Mercy answered with absorbed interest. 'What's the margin of error for interspecies breeding?'

'On average, ninety-five percent of embryos are rejected during gestation.

But we've achieved up to thirty-five percent success rate at the blastula stage, which helps us understand gene expression for further modifications and genetic reprogramming.'

'Is there any fear the human donors will accidentally encounter a hybrid recognisable as themselves?'

'The animal DNA should modify physical attributes sufficiently, even at C2 levels. But we also randomise human feature activation using recessive gene traits to generate variation as an extra precaution.'

*Shwoop.* Chase led Mercy through another sealed door.

The Incubation Room permanently sat at a perfect thirty-seven degrees Celsius. Petri dishes emerging through the opening in the wall funnelled down the belt to a hose hanging overhead. The microscopic eggs were sucked up and sent looping through transparent tubes into one of the thousands of oval glass containers hanging from a vast metal grid stretching over two thousand feet in all directions. A further series of tubes chasing the giant grid structure pulsated synthetic blood into the vases and further into thinner veins lining the pink, fleshy placenta suspended in an amniotic liquid.

*Thump...thump...thump.* The rhythm and sound replicating a human heart reverberated through the room. Chase came to a sudden stop, causing Mercy to almost bump into him.

'Listen,' he commanded.

The heartbeat accelerated; *thump, thump, thump, thump.* Moments later, it slowed to a steady *thump...thump...thump.*

'The artificial heartbeat and blood flow replicate variations in speed experienced in humans during different emotional states from joy to fear to wake and sleep. We've found the embryos adjust better after birth when exposed to a similar gestation environment to human incubation, which is never consistent.'

The pods filled with foetuses in varying stages of gestation were organised by week. Week one – first five rows; week two – sixth, seventh and eighth rows; and on it went for nine months down the hall.

Chase walked Mercy past the various stages of life, explaining the criteria used to govern termination protocols.

'Here, we monitor daily cell growth. Each week, those that pass move down the hall,' he shared as busy white metal robot arms zipped along the grid scanning the tiny life forms. Iridescent green lasers rolled up and down the canisters.

They arrived at the five-week rows when the embryos still resembled the ancient fish body of our common ancestors. A light above a pod near Mercy blinked red. With a clank, the vessel released from the plastic lifeline and dropped through a perfectly shaped opening in the ground, disappearing.

'What happened to that pod?' Mercy asked, interrupting Chase while he explained the antiballistic humidification method that discouraged antibacterial growth.

'Which pod?' he asked, not having noticed the disposal.

'That pod. It dropped down that hole.'

'Terminated,' Chase said casually. 'Could be a host of reasons: malformed embryo, complete regression to recessive traits, or exhibiting features beyond C10 classification...'

The impersonal measure of death left Mercy cold. 'Chase, where are the doctors?'

'They're upstairs, monitoring the system.'

'But what if there is a mistake in the assessment? Or the foetuses could be saved?'

He answered with brutal honesty. 'Exactly. What if? Would you want to carry the burden of knowing? We keep humans and Chimeras out of termination protocols. Better that way for all involved.

'Our timing is good; there's a birthing session about to happen,' continued Chase, leading her through the next door.

A loud whoosh and then a splash announced the draining of the embryotic fluids from the glass wombs. Tiny wrinkled newborns coated in combinations of fur and pink flesh lay in pristine white medical carts as doctors moved methodically, lifting them upside down by the ankles and clearing their mouths of any restrictive fluids. Umbilical cords were cut, and the lab-grown placentas sent down blood-lined drains to be recycled.

Mercy stood behind the railing of the observation balcony listening to the cacophony of infant bawlings.

'Their cries,' she observed out loud, 'They're all different.'

'Yes, it depends on the hybrid. It's never the same. But all infants cry for their mothers.'

Mercy thought she detected a sadness in his voice.

The medical carts, now filled with the unusual creatures cleaned and calm, moved onto the transport belt to be escorted to the rearing barracks on floors above ground. From that point, life for the infants was regimented: intense physical and intellectual training, the finest foods, and top teachers. The Prime felt it was important that hybrids showed their best potential both in physical and mental abilities.

'We can have lunch with the students if you'd like,' Chase invited.

'Very much,' Mercy replied, genuinely awestruck by the enormity of the program.

The cafeteria on floor thirteen buzzed with children Chimeras sitting orderly at long refectory tables wearing black bodysuit uniforms. Unmoved by the visitors entering the room, they argued about genetic theory and mathematical equations where other children might discuss games and gossip as they ingested their plant-based meals. Animal food products were outlawed in the Sanctuary with the birth of hybrids.

Chase and Mercy sat at a small round table reserved for caregivers and instructors. It overlooked an outside balcony where Chimera children were practising physical drills from gymnastics to martial arts to track and yoga.

'Regiment Ten-Twenty entering,' came a voice over the loudspeaker. The children in the cafeteria fell silent on command. A group of ten Chimeras around the age of fifteen marched in, stopping short of the food line. Everyone in the room put a hand to chest over heart as Regiment Ten-Twenty recited in unison: 'For the miracle, we are blessed. For the future, we will not rest. We are grateful. We are strong. Mind and body, we belong. All hail the Prime!'

The newly arrived students broke formation and hurried to the buffet. The others launched back into a heated discussion.

Private Theo's use of the words *Children of the Miracle* popped into Mercy's mind.

'Today we have successfully birthed thousands of hybrids…' Chase continued; unaware she wasn't listening.

Mercy interrupted, 'That pledge they recite, is it mandatory?'

'In school, yes.'

'Miracle?' she questioned hesitantly. 'What part does divinity play in the science of Chimeras?'

'You mustn't think of it in terms of ancient religions. The reference is more to remind Chimeras and humans alike of a time when they didn't know how to stop the FossilFlu. Calling hybrid science a miracle brings a higher reverence to the remarkable scientific development that brought a solution to human extinction. I think that warrants a god-like reference, don't you?'

'Are you referring to the Chimeras or the Prime?' Mercy smiled.

'Maybe a little of both,' quipped Chase, playing along.

Mercy was still thinking of the avian girl. 'Chase, has there been any testing of non-mammalian hybrids?'

He lowered his voice. 'Yes, in the beginning. A few foetuses were brought to term and even raised into young childhood. But brain development was an issue. They displayed highly aggressive behaviours with no ability to control primal instincts. Skeletal structure and reproductive organs were other issues. We couldn't develop species with functioning legs, arms, thumbs and sex organs similar enough to human form, making it difficult for them to fit into society without significant modifications. But the major issue was communication: the ability to make human vocal sounds and use higher-level syntax in communication remained unresolved. Non-mammalian hybrid testing was outlawed, and the subjects terminated.'

Mercy hesitated, considered all options, and took a leap of faith. 'I think I've seen one.'

Chase stared at her without reaction, which unnerved her.

She continued hurriedly, 'It visited my apartment last night. I think it was a human-avian hybrid. It had wings, a beak and four large hooked claws instead of nails on her feet. But otherwise, she had a distinctly human skeleton.' Mercy's speech quickened; she tried to hold her voice down. 'The child sang to me – well, whistling, like a bird, in response to questions.'

'Impossible,' Chase abruptly closed any possibility for consideration. 'Look, I think I know what's happening. When hybrids first entered society, no longer just an experiment in a lab, some people reported being stalked – hybrids trying to kill them. The claims were always proven to be false, even though they insisted the events and animals were real. The hallucinations are a psychosis born from a human prey instinct to protect oneself. It's not uncommon in the beginning, when you first experience Chimeras, to have trouble making sense of them. You must have imagined the creature.'

Mercy felt a wave of relief hearing Chase's logical explanation. *Yes, of course. It was just a dream.* And maybe she had misheard the hooded stranger as well. *Danger? No, no danger, after all.*

# CHAPTER THIRTEEN

Mercy awoke excited, after a strong start to the research project, having a full day to explore the Green Belt. They would start the trip to the Belt by flying up to the Northern mountains, heading down the valley and have a late lunch in a wild grass prairie on the edge of a pine forest.

Punctually at nine o'clock, she arrived at the docking bay. Chase and Joan were waiting for her. They climbed into the ship and started at once.

Immediately outside the city's northern wall, successive rows of vegetable and fruit crops stretched for miles. Large drone farming machines steadily moved up and down the patchwork of lush orchards and abundant crops while farmworkers in sterilized yellow uniforms watched over the constant harvest.

Within the hour they had passed over the Agricultural Zone and entered the high plains, an unending expanse of flat earth covered in prairie, steppe and grasslands. Herds of buffalo, deer and wild horses slowly migrated south, their well-worn trails like black tendrils stretching out and twining across the earth.

By noon the flat prairies had broken into undulating black hills covered in dense pine forests like a shadow cast over the land. Mountain rivers cut through the canopy, their white rapids raging down steep banked valleys, bubbling over rocky beds.

Less than an hour further north, after passing over a wildflower valley, they finally arrived at a glacial mountain range. A towering spine of snow-capped peaks pushed up from the horizon. Puff pastry white clouds glided along the sharp razor edge of black rock, creating a parade of nebulous shapes on a conveyor belt of wind.

Mercy fell back into her chair in awe and delight at the majestic views.

Jane came to a hover beside a thundering waterfall, cut deep into the mountainside. Torrents of white water cascaded down the rocky gorge, so loud they could hardly hear their breathing. Drawing closer, they entered the clouds of vapour that hung over the swirling pool where the vertical river crashed into the ground. Water washed over their heads and down the sides of the ship like sitting under an invisible umbrella. At the edge of the pool, the ice-cold snowmelt narrowed into the start of a roaring river, carving down the foothills until disappearing into a forested valley.

Joan turned the ship back in the direction they had arrived and followed the river down to the forest's edge. She landed near the river's pebbled shoreline where they would have lunch.

Outside, the damp air of the mountain's breath brushed against Mercy. Her face glowed with pleasure. The soft sounds of the burbling stream drew her in. She bent and put a hand in the freezing water and smiled. Spontaneously, she removed her shoes and walked ankle-deep into the shallows; pimpled flesh lined her cold legs as her bare feet pressed into the silky soft sand. Reaching down, she scooped the spring waters up and splashed her face, laughing at the pleasure of prickling needles along her cheeks.

To excited to eat, Mercy convinced Joan and Chase to start with a hike. Strolling along the riverbank Chase described the plants and creatures of the valley with great enthusiasm: grasses, wildflowers, insects, rodents, predators and prey.

Mercy had an insatiable desire to touch and smell everything. She felt they were moving too quickly. She asked if she could continue as they prepared lunch. Joan reluctantly agreed.

Mercy walked for some way into the forest, eager to stand below the treetops. Joan and Chase's voices faded, replaced by the trills and tweets of mountain birds. Dappled sunlight danced on the forest floor, and the world around her grew thick with woods, bushes and ferns.

The sudden solitude excited her senses and sent her mind racing with imaginings. She felt savage. A brisk movement behind a low-lying tree could be a wolf. The crack of a dry branch could be a bear hunting. Each imagined threat raised the drumbeat of her heart so loud she almost missed the warning hum of a coming Solar Wave.

Her ears tickled. Suddenly hidden animals from every direction broke out in concert, hooting, thrumming, chirping and buzzing in anticipation. The forest animals sang for the sunshine, and it was delivered in a flash of white light raining down on the canopy, combing through the pine trees, brushing over the ferns and fungi, and chasing the shadows of the forest floor aside for a brief moment. Closing her eyes, Mercy breathed in the intoxicating release of fresh oxygen.

*Snap* – something light and small broke overhead, falling on her. Without warning, branches and leaves started raining down on her. She looked up towards a loud flapping noise coming from the trees and gasped. She was not alone. Perched on a branch high above her sat the avian child from her dreams.

The girl let out a shrill cry and pointed her wing-arm to Mercy's left.

Mercy heard the predator before she saw it. Branches on the ground were breaking, moving in her direction. A bone-vibrating roar and the thump of heavy feet slapping the earth announced a colossal black bear.

Two steps backwards, a stumble, and she was on her backside. Quickly scurrying, she tried to upright herself and escape, but it was too late. Standing on his hind legs, the bear let out a thunderous roar, before surging forward.

Mercy quickly felt the ground for something to protect herself and found a large stone, fingers gripping automatically.

His was the first contact, slicing her chest with razor-sharp claws. Mercy shrieked; the pain of torn flesh burned.

Hers was the next strike. Stone in hand, she swiped with all her strength at his exposed skull. *Crack!* Something broke, something important. The bear reeled backwards, disoriented. But her victory was short. He found his footing and turned back on her. Loose skin undulated under his belly as he lunged into the air and landed on her.

The last thing Mercy saw was the mad stare of a killer's eyes. The last thing Mercy heard was the growl of another animal from behind. Her world went black.

# CHAPTER FOURTEEN

'Mercy? It's Chase. Can you hear me?'

He held her hand as the ship sped back to Sanctuary City with Joan at the helm. Mercy opened her eyes and blinked. A fog started clearing from her mind.

'What…happened?' her words were slow and staggered. She tried to sit up, which caused her head to go fizzy.

'Woah,' coached a worried Chase, gently pressing her shoulders backwards, leaving her prone on the levitating emergency gurney. 'You need to stay down. That bear seriously injured you.'

Mercy touched the gauze wrapped tightly around her chest.

'We've treated your cut. It's healed now, but you will feel bruised for a while.'

Her thoughts and words became more lucid. 'I remember hitting the bear on the head, and then he jumped at me. I was certain I was going to die.' Her voice drifted off as she noticed the bandage wrapped around Chase's right shoulder. 'Chase, what happened to your arm?'

Chase ignored the question. 'You'll be fine now. I've given you a mild sedative. The doctor is waiting for you in your apartment.' His words dragged out, getting longer and slower until his face faded away.

The next morning, Mercy could move more freely. Her injuries had turned from crippling soreness to mild discomfort overnight.

Joan had stopped by Mercy's apartment. There was a new casualness to their relationship since the trip to the Belt. Not old friends, but friendlier than acquaintances. Mercy welcomed the company.

'Everyone has taken a great interest in your recovery. The Prime, the Senators, and your Agent Basil,' shared Joan, placing a full cup of hot coffee on the table near Mercy.

'And Doctor Chase?'

Joan tilted her head quizzically, 'Yes, Doctor Chase as well.'

'No, I mean, I'm grateful he's concerned, but how is he doing? What happened to his shoulder?'

'He found you in the woods after we heard your scream. I couldn't keep up. By the time I arrived, he was carrying you back to the ship. Both of you were injured.'

Hope interrupted, 'Doctor Mercy, you have a visitor. Doctor Chase is outside.'

Joan got up from the table. 'Busy morning,' she smiled. 'Your schedule has been updated with Hope. You have as much time as you need to recover. I'll let the Prime and Agent Basil know you're doing well.'

'You can let her know I'll be back in the lab today,' Mercy directed, not waiting for a response. 'I'm fine now.'

'As you wish.' Joan paused before leaving, 'If you're up for it, there's an Aurora Carnival tonight. Two times a year, we let enough sun into the upper atmosphere to create a firework display of colours across the Shade. It might be a nice break for you. I've left the invitation on your schedule.'

'Thank you, Joan,' Mercy said in a sincere and personal tone as Joan turned to leave. 'Hope, let Doctor Chase in.'

The door slid open. Joan and Chase acknowledged each other as they passed. Mercy crept off her chair, painfully standing to welcome Chase.

'No, you need to stay down,' he insisted, finger waving in the air as if commanding a child.

'I'm fine now,' insisted Mercy as she took her seat. Her gaze went to his shoulder. The bandage, if on, was covered by his uniform. 'How's your arm?'

'All good,' he smiled. An awkward moment of silence revealed he had not thought through his visit.

Mercy rescued him. 'Chase, I think I owe you a large debt of gratitude. What happened after I blacked out?'

His eyes shuffled, trying to avoid something. 'I found you just as the bear had pinned you down. We wrestled, and it ran off.'

'I can't thank you enough.'

'Please don't. Besides,' Chase smiled again, 'I think you pretty much took care of it yourself. That injury to his head took the fight out of him. Impressive right.'

Mercy blushed. Now the awkward silence was hers. She glanced away nervously, wondering if she should tell him everything that had happened. Surely she could trust a man who had saved her life. 'Chase, I saw it again. The avian hybrid. She was up in a tree, trying to warn me about the bear.'

'Mercy, you were scared. A wild animal was stalking you. It's not unreasonable that you imagined her.'

'Why do you insist on doubting me?' She was getting more and more frustrated.

Chase gently held her wrist. 'Calm down. I do not doubt that you saw something. But an avian hybrid is just not possible. If one did exist, it would be terminated. That's the law. And Mercy, you need to stop talking about this.'

Chase walked over to the sink, turned on the faucet and waved for her to join him. He placed her wrist with the band under the running water.

His voice changed low and secretive. 'Even if this creature did exist, you must not get involved. The Purists would have it destroyed, and if you helped in any way, they would charge you. Non-mammalian hybridisation is a serious matter. Do you understand me?'

Mercy's heart sped up. 'What are you saying? Am I in danger?'

'No. That's what I'm trying to avoid,' he pleaded. Chase's eyes followed hers. 'Let's just get back to work, and you can soon return home safely.'

His hand held her thin, bald wrist, as the warm water rushed over their pressed flesh. Something moved through them, broke Chase, and he couldn't hold back.

'I was so worried,' he confessed, almost in tears, 'when I saw you under that bear. I thought you were already gone. And it was my fault.'

'Your fault? I went into the woods alone.'

'But I let you go...' Chase's voice drifted. His expression suddenly changed. Cheeks flushed with desire, pupils wide and imploring, and ears tucked back, he leaned in with lips parted.

Mercy quickly pulled back, startled.

A dark shadow transformed Chase's nature. He looked down on her, hurt, and humiliated. 'I'm sorry,' he said in a voice so profoundly ashamed, that Mercy felt sad for him. Chase turned and quickly ran out of the room.

She stood alone, dumbstruck, holding her quivering wrist. She could still feel the pleasure of Chase's touch against her skin.

*But he's not human!*

# CHAPTER FIFTEEN

Mercy was trapped. After the terrifying experience in the forest, and now Chase's confession of his personal feelings, she didn't know which way to turn.

The words of the stranger in the hall began to haunt her once again, *'You're in danger.'* She thought about leaving the Sanctuary but quickly dismissed the idea as childish. No, she was much stronger than that. At the very least she should send Agent Basil a message to water her tree, she thought. But what would she tell him? Other than a stranger's threat, there were no signs of danger. And the bear attack was her fault. If she were going to contact Agent Basil, she would need something more substantive.

'Hope, pull up the report on MUTATION FFv1 ANTI-SPARG3. Have lab PVA run a full analysis of the viral mutation post antidote testing. I'm looking for anomalies that may have surfaced but were not pertinent to results. I want to see everything.'

The morning quickly passed as Mercy filed through reams of data, looking for anything unusual, and updating the search criteria in real-time. It was like looking for a snowflake in an avalanche, but this is what she excelled at: finding what others couldn't.

By late afternoon, ready to give up for the day, Hope announced a breakthrough. 'Doctor Mercy, the lab PVA, has run the current analysis. There is a change of nucleotide bases in the viral genome which match your criteria. The results indicate there is a forty-two percent probability of genetic modification using biotechnologies.'

Mercy sat back in her chair; eyes worried. Genetic engineering was only a hunch, one of several theories. But this was the one theory she desperately hoped was not true.

*Why would someone engineer the mutation and who?* She asked herself. Mercy needed absolute certainty before going to the Prime, and that meant getting into the lab and running tests on the live virus. But only a few scientists had access.

Mercy took a deep breath. 'Hope, please call Doctor Chase.'

The holographic display lit up in Mercy's apartment, and an image of Chase sitting at his desk appeared.

'Doctor Mercy, how can I help?' His tone was distant.

Mercy expected awkwardness but calling her by her professional title after everything they had been through together hurt. An air of something ending hung between them in a moment of silence, a door closing before fully opened.

'Hello, Chase.' Her voice was friendly. 'I'd like to ask for permission to run some tests on the live virus.'

Chase offered a blank stare. 'Why?'

'I have an idea about a possible antigen,' she lied.

'We run all theories through simulation first, before live testing. I'm sure you can appreciate the extreme safety protocols around the virus. We are under strict orders to limit all unnecessary access.'

'I understand,' Mercy plotted quickly, 'But I'm only here for a limited time. If I spend all my time in simulations, it will delay any real progress.'

Chase thought silently before answering. 'Okay, I'll set it up for tomorrow morning. There are protocols. But it shouldn't be a problem. Can you submit your theory by the end of the day?'

'I'll have Hope send through the details of the tests right now.'

'That should be enough. I'll set up the lab time.' His response rushed, ready to end the conversation.

'Thank you,' said Mercy, wanting to say more, wanting to fix the mornings uncomfortable events.

The illumination of Chase disappeared.

Mercy anxiously tapped her finger on the table, unable to relax. She desperately needed to get her mind off of Chase and the virus. 'Hope, let Ambassador Joan know I'll be joining her for the celebration tonight.'

# CHAPTER SIXTEEN

An enormous and grand garden grew on the rooftop of the White Tower.

Tall grasses, stem roses framed in boxed shrubs, and giant palm trees quilted five imposing boulevards stretching the length of the Sky Park. At the centre of the rooftop garden, cascading sheets of water fell from a thin metal disk levitating two stories high and landed in a palatial pond. Four troughs, in the form of a cross, ushered the water to the park's boundaryless edges, where the silver rivers disappeared into the skyline.

A live orchestra played from a large bandshell near the end of the park. Politicians and business elites gathered in tiny herds, politely smiling and socialising, glasses of champagne and wine in hand.

Mercy arrived, dressed in the tunic for public affairs. She looked around for Joan as she accepted a glass of champagne from a roving waitress. The Sanctuary's ritual of drinking in the evenings had grown on her quickly.

In a nearby corner of the garden, Joan stood with Senator Arjun. The Senator was angrily jabbing a sharp finger in Joan's direction. Joan remained calm, taking the virtual punches without reaction. She said something in response; something the Senator clearly didn't like. His poxy face turned a bright red, eyes bulged, and nose jutted towards her as he moved in to reiterate his point. Joan glanced over her shoulder and spotted Mercy. Politely putting a hand in the air, she excused herself, leaving him shaking with fury. He immediately spun on his heels and stormed away.

'The Senator seemed upset?' Mercy felt the question acceptable between new friends.

'Senator Arjun would like a private meeting with you. I've told him the

Prime would need to approve it.'

'Me, why?' Mercy sounded surprised.

'He wouldn't say. Well, he said it was above my rank and how dare I question him,' Joan shrugged her shoulders. 'Don't worry about it. I'll let the Prime know, and they can sort it out between themselves.'

'Is everything okay? Did I do something wrong?'

Joan placed a hand on Mercy's back and turned her towards the Northern sky. 'Mercy, don't worry about Senator Arjun. His problems shouldn't concern you. Now, watch this...'

A familiar low reverberating metal drumming shook her bones as the Solar Wave approached.

'The Aurora is about to start,' announced Joan, her eyes lit with excitement.

The entire balcony of partygoers went silent. The band stopped playing. Anticipation was heavy and infectious as people started gathering around the garden's infinity edge. Roars of celebration suddenly rang out from the city behind the Tower where the Aurora had already begun.

Mercy caught first sight of the spectacle as the crowd around her began *oohing* and *ahhing*. Faint streaks of green and white light crept across the sky, growing more intense with each vibration of the Solar Wave. Suddenly, the green lights turned to blood-red rivers racing over their heads, followed by a tidal wave of sapphire blue.

The orchestra burst into sound, delighting the revellers. Music and colour exploded into an otherworldly dance of luminance and mystical songs. It was a spectacle so intense that Mercy could feel the colours under her skin and deep behind her eyes. Her body felt lighter and airy as if she might float.

Twenty minutes later, the lights faded and slowly slipped away as the sky returned to starlit black heaven. The audience burst into applause.

Joan leaned into Mercy's ear and spoke over the noise, 'The public will be celebrating in the city; parades, street dances, it will go on all night. It's not just a beautiful show; it's also a reminder of what the Shade does for us. We celebrate the founders who created the Shade, and we remember to be grateful for the food and nature it provides.'

'Thanks for inviting me,' replied Mercy, her eyes still glowing.

'The Prime has already left for public appearances. We've been invited to join the Senators for dinner if you'd like.'

'And Chase?'

Concern replaced Joan's smile. The two women passed a knowing look between each other that required no words.

After a brief pause, Joan spoke tenderly. 'Be careful Mercy, public tolerance for hybrids hasn't quite caught up with interracial couples. A Pure and a C10 together…well, unofficially, it's still frowned upon by many. It's best not to draw attention to yourself.'

Mercy blushed. 'I…did not mean to suggest…' she stammered, then stopped herself — no point hiding what was becoming apparent. 'Thank you. Understood.'

'Let's head down. We're in private dining,' instructed Joan.

Dinner with the Senators started with obligatory questions and condolences on her accident. 'How unfortunate…' 'It's rare to be attacked in the wild…' 'Nature can be unpredictable…'.

Mercy curiously noted the delicate avoidance of the word 'animal' – *animals can be unpredictable; it's rare animals attack* – statements not made. The subtle choice of wording, or avoiding certain words, defined the difference between animals as hybrids and animals in nature.

As the five-course dinner dragged on, Mercy felt her body and mind grow heavy and tired. Her chest still sore, she excused herself before dessert, requesting to revisit the Sky Park on her own for some fresh air. Joan agreed.

Waiters scurried about the rooftop garden clearing away glasses and plates and tearing down stands. Mercy found a private corner behind the orchestra's stage where she could be alone. Looking out across the bustling city, she couldn't stop herself from thinking of Chase. She imagined him carrying her through the woods, more glamour than blood. Her head pressed against his broad shoulders and chest, weightless in his arms. Perhaps the alcohol clouded her judgement, but she finally gave in to the warm feeling inside. A fantasy started building in her mind where the only part of Chase that mattered was his touch.

*Stop thinking of him!* She ordered herself in vain.

A gust of wind stroked her back.

'Doctor Mercy Perching,' came a deep male voice from behind her.

Mercy spun around and gasped. A full-grown male avian hybrid stood before her. Two large raven-black wings mounted on his back, curved up over his muscular shoulders and rounded downward where wingtips fell below his waist. His feet, uncovered, had scales for skin, and eagle-like talons on his toes. Unlike the bird-child, his face appeared human, except for the yellow irises of his eyes, now piercing through her.

'Who are you,' cried Mercy, gripped with terror.

'You'll know soon enough. We don't have much time. There is a war coming, an army forming, and you are in danger.'

A sudden noise on the far side of the stage caught his attention. He spread his wings.

'What have I got to do with any of this?' she pleaded.

'Trust no one until we talk again. No one,' commanded the bird-man. 'It's not safe here, but we'll meet again.'

His enormous wings outstretched, he eclipsed the horizon behind him. In one powerful thrust, he left the ground and soared up into the air. The sound of beating wings fading away left Mercy standing alone, her heart beating wildly.

# CHAPTER SEVENTEEN

The halls blurred as Mercy raced towards her quarters, heart still punching at her chest after the terrifying encounter with the black-winged man. Careening around the corner of the lobby outside the living quarters, Mercy slammed into Chase. Instinctively he reached out. His firm grip clasped her arms and stopped a nasty fall backwards. Mercy went limp in his embrace, visibly shocked.

'I'm not that scary, am I?' Chase joked, a playful grin on his face.

'Chase, no, of course not.' She unravelled her body from his paws and straightened herself, combing her tossed hair back behind her ears.

'Why the rush?' he asked with a slight slur.

'Chase, have you been drinking?'

'No. Maybe, well a little,' he smiled again, looking a bit unsteady. 'Aurora celebrations, you know.' He tried hard to sound less fuddled.

'Of course,' Mercy nodded and managed a smile in return. 'Okay, so I'll see you tomorrow, then,' she said hurriedly, trying to leave.

'But you see me now,' he joked.

His boyish humour and alcohol-induced honesty forced her to laugh. 'Yes, I do see you.'

'Admit it, I scare you,' he blurted out, his ears rolling backwards, giving her his puppy dog eyes.

'No, you don't,' she insisted, wanting her sincerity to get through his clouded awareness. 'But I do think you need to get to bed. Let me help you.'

Mercy walked Chase around the same corridor three times before he remembered the location of his apartment. She suspected his memory loss was intentional. Chase gave the command to open his door and stepped forward, but immediately spun around on his heels, facing Mercy. 'I bet you thought I couldn't find my apartment.'

Mercy leaned a shoulder up against the outside wall. 'Well, it did seem that way.'

'Maybe I wanted a little more time.'

'Maybe I did too,' her eyes cast down, looking away from him. Her confession surprised her, but she didn't want to be alone.

He leaned in. Mercy put her hand on his chest to hold him at bay. 'Chase, you're inebriated. You don't know what you're doing.'

'Hold that thought.' He ran into his apartment, shuffled around for a few minutes and returned, stable. 'Alcohol metabolising enzymes. I'll be completely sober in five more minutes.'

The boyish grin again. Mercy looked anxious, caught. They stood in silence, close enough to feel each other's body heat without touching. His approaching sobriety returned his more constrained nature.

'But you don't have to stay,' his said a trifle anxiously.

She started to lean towards him but hesitated. He held his position of chivalry, gave her the lead. Her gaze met his piercing blue eyes. Against all the odds and peculiarity of their union, she couldn't understand how, but she wanted him.

He looked up and down the hall, ensuring nobody was around, pulled her into his apartment, and closed the door.

Chase's ears pricked high on his head, and his pupils retracted with intent. He leaned nearer and nearer with lips parted. His breath moved into her first. The warm, moist flesh of his lips against hers sent pleasure down to her bones. He felt as human as any man she had been with before, and desire overtook her mind. She drew him in, each meeting the other's movement with perfect balance. Her cheeks went flush. The kisses grew uncontrollable. Chase pulled away reluctantly, gently holding her hand, and walked her to his bedroom.

Very slowly, with a cautious hand, she started to unbutton his shirt. He looked vulnerable, but his eyes begged her to continue. Suddenly she let out a gasp, pulling away. There, below his brawny male chest, six other nipples lined his abdomen, like a dog.

'Are you nervous?' His question was tender, understanding the source of her resistance.

'Yes,' she answered honestly.

'Don't be. It's the law that all humans and hybrids alike are the same under the belt,' he assured her. Chase held Mercy close, pressing his entire body into hers, revealing his hard, enlarged sameness as all other men.

Mercy's body surged forward. She wanted more but pulled back.

'It's not just that.' Her eyes turned down towards the ground, hesitant. Chase refused to let her drift away.

'Don't worry; I'm sterilised. All C10s are at birth.' He said it matter-of-factly.

'Chase, I'm sorry,' she said tenderly, drawing her face up, meeting his eyes. 'I didn't mean to say…I mean, that doesn't sound fair.'

'Don't worry about me. Besides,' he continued light of heart, 'it means we can have more fun.'

He grinned boyishly and held her close. Wrapping her arms around his sinewy back, she felt a strip of fur on his spine, stretching from the base of his neck to his firm buttocks. She stroked the dense fur undercoat covered in coarse, thick overhairs. He arched in pleasure, pressing his chest even harder into hers, his kiss more intense.

They lay on his bed, undressed, and became one. Chase moved inside her and gently rocked with pleasure. Mercy arched her back, meeting the ebb and tide of his thrust. Twenty minutes passed as if seconds. His heart beat faster, and his pace quickened. Lips curled back he let out a growl, exposing his sharp incisors, designed for killing and protecting in equal measure. His blades aroused Mercy as one final push from Chase released both their final desires simultaneously. They remained twisted as one, collapsed in a heap of flesh and fur.

Chase rolled his ears back, breathed heavily on her chest, and held her close. She was his, part of his pack, a bond deep and old, instinctive.

Mercy allowed herself to be treasured but privately wondered if she had made the right choice. These thoughts could wait until the morning, she told herself. For tonight, she felt safe again, and she slipped into a much-needed sleep.

# CHAPTER EIGHTEEN

Mercy woke to the sounds of Chase opening his closet.

'Sorry, I've slept in.' She offered, pulling herself into a sitting position — a dream of something already forgotten left a strange melancholy.

'It's still early. But you'll need to get up soon. I have you scheduled for live culture testing. I'm sure you'll want to get a head start.'

'Yes, of course,' replied Mercy slightly taken back by his abrupt dismissal.

Chase read her mind, jumped on the bed, hovered over her on all fours and jokingly barked, a terrible human imitation of a dog's bark at that. Mercy cringed.

'Too soon?' quipped Chase.

'Yes,' she laughed, pushing him aside, 'too soon.'

'Let me show you Sanctuary City tonight,' he pleaded. 'You can't go back without seeing everything.'

The words 'go back' hurt her. 'Chase, I don't think it's wise. I'm not here for fun. And won't it draw unnecessary attention?'

His brow melted into sadness. The words 'draw attention' hurt him. Mercy wanted to apologise, instantly take it back.

He pondered, 'Probably right.' Lifting himself off the bed, he continued dressing. 'So...let's invite Ambassador Joan,' he smirked, 'make it an official trip, a cultural education.'

He retrieved trousers from the closet and slipped them on. Mercy felt a surge of lust on seeing his firm backside clench as he pulled his pants up.

'Yes, I would like to see the city,' she teased.

He looked over his shoulder at her, waiting.

'– with you,' she conceded, flirting awkwardly.

Pleased with her response, he signalled the beginning of their morning. 'Right, serious matters ahead,' he announced stone-faced as if their time together had gone on too long.

The Infectious Disease Facility resided on floor minus thirty, deep below the old city, built before the days of sun control. The sign overhead read DANGER. BIOHAZARD. AUTHORISED PERSONNEL ONLY. Behind heavy surveillance, reinforced steel doors, and a hermetically sealed ceramic barrier, sixty-foot-long freezers lined the outer walls of the vast two-storey-tall bunker. Inside the cold storage units, shelved and filed diseases filled rows upon rows of glass tubes, labelled and laid to rest under fluorescent green lights; frozen in cryogenic infinity.

High on the west-facing wall, behind a thick protective window, and under a cold dead light, Mercy stood looking down on the storage lab. In the centre of the room, trays of empty glass test tubes, microwaves, and gyroscopic mixers sat on steel tables. Nearby, parked in holding ramps, twenty robotic arms, able to perform precise surgical movements, sat waiting for instruction.

Mercy's lab assistant, a raccoon-woman with bandit's eyes, waved her hand in the air. A virtual control centre activated over the giant window. Below them, the lab had suddenly come to life. Bright lights lit up over the tables, and the robots levitated off their stands, fingers pointed upward as if in a salute. After a brief introduction to the system, Mercy placed her hands into the holographic panel and started moving the mechanical assistants below.

The hours passed quickly. Morning turned to an early night. Mercy made faster progress than she had expected but still didn't have the answers she needed.

'Doctor Mercy, you have one hour before dinner with Ambassador Joan and Doctor Chase in Sanctuary City,' interrupted Hope.

Mercy let out a profound sigh, stretched her arms over her head, and took a step away from the control panel.

'Well, I'm almost done here,' she announced reluctantly. 'I've given further instruction to lab PVA, which should keep it busy through the night,' she shared with the racoon-woman assistant.

The assistant nodded, her pricked silver ears twitched. 'You'll be notified as soon as the results come in, Doctor.'

Mercy thanked her and headed back to her quarters to prepare for dinner with Chase and Joan.

84

# CHAPTER NINETEEN

Middle Town was recovered from the remnants of the original Sanctuary City, before the Scorch and Shade. Built on ground level; it separated Upper and Lower Towns. It's brick and stone buildings, scarred by centuries of urban decay, housed restaurants, bars, and clubs of various repute.

On the streets, crowds of Human and Chimera revellers weaved through the colourful markets and mingled outside hovering food carts. Larger-than-life holographic billboards, lit in neon-lights, tussled for their attention offering temptations of food, drink, and fun.

Overhead, strung like spider webs from building to building, layers of glass travellators pulsated with eager party goers and joy seekers abandoned to the evening.

Inside, the restaurant was bustling. Dinner with Joan and Chase neared an end. Mercy was relieved to have finished without incident. Chase snuck a few secret glances, and she reciprocated with a knowing grin and scolding shake of her head. But overall, nobody seemed to catch on to their affair; not even Joan.

As the waiter served the last of the wine, the mood shifted. Chase caught Joan's eye and nodded towards her. She raised one eyebrow, uncertain. After a few moments, she pushed her wine glass away and leaned into the table towards Mercy, secretive.

'Mercy, I shouldn't be telling you this. But Chase believes you deserve to know the details behind your invitation to come to the Sanctuary. What I'm sharing with you needs to stay between us.'

Chase looked relieved.

'Okay?' Mercy replied hesitantly.

'Senator Arjun requested that we alert your Sanctuary about the mutation. Not the Prime.'

'Excuse me?' Sobriety hit Mercy with a thud.

'Senator Arjun, for some time now, has argued for open diplomacy with your country. As I've shared before, his party, the Purists, believe hybrid technology goes against nature. They have a minority in the Senate, and he needs alliances – like your government. He refers to you as untainted bloodlines. He believes he can build his influence here at home with a broader international coalition.'

'I don't know what to say...' Mercy's voice trailed off in astonishment. No words came that could express her growing anger. How dare the Senator assume she would be any part of a plan to eradicate people like Chase and Joan.

Joan spoke earnestly. 'The Prime finally agreed, but with restrictions. The invitation would be for you alone, giving her a chance to introduce you to the Chimeras, and hopefully build an ally. You can now understand why Senator Arjun is so keen to meet you and why I've held back.'

'So, the Prime doesn't want me here at all. That's what you're saying?'

'No, that's not what I'm saying. The Prime genuinely believes you can help us find a cure, but has made it clear to Chase and me, we're to keep you out of our politics. The mutation of FossilFlu cast doubt on the hybrid program and gave Arjun the impetus he needed to raise enough votes and force the Prime's hand. Her hesitation was about protecting us, the Chimeras.'

'*War is coming. You're in danger.*' The avian man's words rang in her head. A chill shook her shoulders. She had an urge to tell Chase and Joan about the avian man and his haunting message, but something held her back. '*Trust no one.*'

Chase tried to reassure her. 'It doesn't matter now. We just wanted you to understand and to trust us. You and me, what we're doing here, working together to stop FossilFlu, that's the important thing. We're scientists, not politicians.'

Mercy remained silent, contemplative.

Chase glanced down at the table. 'Perhaps we shouldn't have told you.'

'No, I'm glad you did,' Mercy finally acknowledged, giving Chase the answer he wanted. 'You're right. It doesn't matter. All that matters is the cure.'

Desperate to break the sour mood, Chase smiled and slapped a paw on the table. 'Let's move this conversation on, shall we? I'd like you to see the Orchard before we call it a night. Will you join us for one drink?'

Joan looked annoyed. 'Chase, I'm not sure that's a good idea.'

'What's the Orchard?' Mercy welcomed the change of conversation.

'Sort of an evening club,' he explained.

'It's a competition bar,' Joan told Mercy in a warning tone. 'Hybrids challenge each other to physical matches, using their animal skills to outmanoeuvre their opponent. The clubs are frowned upon by most.'

'It's one of the only places where being more than a human is better,' Chase argued, his tone full of bravado and alpha positioning.

Joan shook her head in disparagement.

'Okay,' he conceded, 'It's not exactly a diplomatic destination, but it's harmless fun.'

Mercy understood. He wanted her to be a part of his life, if only for a night. 'Joan, with your permission?' she asked.

'You're a free person here, Mercy, not our prisoner. We will do as you like,' Joan sounded sincere. 'However, I am responsible for your safety, and I thought it best to explain what you're getting into.'

Chase chimed in, 'Ambassador Joan doesn't like going to fight clubs. Most humans and C2s don't,' he smirked accusingly. 'But I bet she's been to a few,' he teased.

Joan spoke with stern eyes, 'This is not about me.'

'Very well, then,' Chase claimed his victory. 'I'll call a drone.'

# CHAPTER TWENTY

A tin sign swung on a metal arm with the words THE ORCHARD cut through. In small print below it said: All Hybrids Welcome. Waiting underneath the invitation, Chimeras of every make queued impatiently to get in.

Chase walked to the front of the line with no apology and spoke to the doorman, a massive burly bear-man hybrid, who immediately ushered the three of them in ahead of the annoyed onlookers.

They stepped through the dark entrance and found themselves on a circular balcony overlooking a pit. Neon strobe lights wove through the crowds of Chimeras stacked layers deep up to the balcony's edge. Syncopated hypnotic rhythms pulsed through the air as mechanical drumbeats punched up from the metal floor. Gyrating crowds of human bodies with animal parts, dressed in digital bodysuits with oscillating colours, danced on the pit floor.

'I've had a table arranged. We're over here,' Chase shouted over the music, guiding Mercy and Joan to a private box seat at the edge of the balcony. 'I'll grab us drinks,' he shouted again and disappeared down the stairs.

Mercy felt the eyes of the room uncomfortably on her as they sat in the exclusive area. 'Are we being watched?' she asked, leaning close to Joan so as not to have to scream.

'We are. The Pure and High-Cs don't usually come here. Not when the entertainment starts,' answered Joan.

A sudden intense drum roll silenced the crowd. The room went black, and a single spotlight burst on a doorway in the pit. A wolf-man hybrid emerged, pumping his paw-hands in the air. Tufts of grey fur smuggled their way out of the sleeves of his sparkling red bodysuit. Naked from throat to navel, his muscular chest and rippled abdomen were on display.

The crowds erupted in cheers. The wolf climbed into one of two cages hanging in the pit, carried forward by the hoots and jeers of his audience.

'Hooowl!' He roared in a fevered pitch to the audiences dancing around his cage, delighted as they barked in return.

Chase reappeared. 'Just in time,' he whispered, handing the drinks over and sitting next to Mercy.

'Ladies, gentlemen, and...well the rest of you – ANIMALS!' trumpeted an invisible voice from the speakers, causing excitement to flare up and ripple through the room.

With a thud, a black-suited and top-hatted feline hybrid landed onto the central podium elevated between two cages in the middle of the pit. Stretching his Cheshire cat smile and arms wide the ringmaster sang out, 'Tonight, for your entertainment, we have the ever-popular Predator versus Prey.'

The crowd roared and pumped their fists into the air, chanting, 'Kill! Kill! Kill!'

Mercy glanced at Chase with startled eyes.

'Welcome, please, to my right, the dancing wolf from district two, Rameses,' bellowed the cat-man.

The wolf-man climbed into one of the cages and vigorously shook the bars, growled, and curled his lips, exposing large menacing canines.

The audience egged him on. 'Predator! Predator! Predator!'

'And to my left,' the ringmaster waved an arm as a spotlight snapped onto the second cage, 'Welcome the Trojan horse, the thoroughbred from district five, Adelaide!'

The body of the woman who now stepped out into the spotlight was more horse than human; her swollen glutes and thick thighs balanced on stick-thin shins and hooves separated into five appendages like toes. Her straight, coarse, black hair hung in a ponytail past her waist. Her human skull stretched long and thin, spreading her eyes wide so that they were nearly on her temples.

As the cage door closed her in, she fiercely bobbed her head at the wolf-man, letting loose a neigh and a whinny, slamming her hoof toes on the metal floor.

Mercy shifted uncomfortably in her seat. 'Chase? I'm not sure...'

Chase raised his hand, 'Wait,' he said calmly with a knowing grin, reassuring her.

A loud clack started the chains rolling up, lifting the cages off the ground.

The ringmaster addressed the two contestants. 'You know the rules. A wound ends the set; a kill ends the match. When the bell rings, time is up. The winner becomes…' he raised a golden crown high into the air as the audience finished his sentence, '…THE KING OF THE JUNGLE!' The cat whirled around and sprang off his platform into the darkness. His voice sang out over the speakers: 'READY…TO…RUMBLE…IN…THE…JUNGLE!'

Enormous shafts of light shot up through the metal cages, swallowing the wolf and horse into a golden halo.

'Prey gets the first choice,' announced the ringmaster.

The horse-woman yelled, 'Savannah,' to crowd cheers.

The contestants suddenly transported into a holographic semi-arid desert plain but in different locations.

Chase smiled broadly at Mercy. 'You see, it's only virtual. We may be more animal than human, but we aren't savages,' he laughed.

Mercy's shoulders fell as she dropped slowly back into her chair and smiled.

The wolf-man stood in tall waving grass under a bright blue sky, facing the open flatlands that stretched beyond the border of his hiding place. In the distance, the horse-woman came into sight, running towards a large body of water (extra points gained for stocking up on supplies during a game). A palpable stillness hung over the audience in anticipation.

Slowly, the wolf-man started to slink through the grass, gradually picking up pace, his eyes locked on his prey. Faster he ran, lighter on foot, until he broke free from his hiding place at full speed. Breathing heavily, pushing hard, he raced to cut the horse-woman off from her water source. She ran faster than him, in a full gallop, but quicker to tire. As she slowed, he closed in, cut her off. She slid to a dramatic stop, dust clouds rolling up around her feet.

'Bring it on!' she shouted to the audience's delight.

Her long black mane swayed from side to side as she pawed at the ground with her virtual hooves replacing her human feet. The wolf leapt an impossible height into the air. The horse spun around and bolted in the opposite direction. The slap of the wolf's body crashing down onto her backend caused howls and hoots from the audience. His virtual claws sunk into her flesh and blood let, squirting outside the virtual boundaries onto delighted onlookers.

It all seemed over when suddenly she retaliated with a forceful backward kick, striking him in the groin, sending him flying in the direction he charged.

The men in the audience grimaced, the women cheered. Mercy, captivated, leapt upward in her seat at the blow.

The savannah suddenly evaporated, leaving both contenders licking their virtual wounds. 'Round one, tie,' shouted the ringmaster over the loudspeaker. 'Round two, Predator's call.'

The wolf-man danced in one spot, jumping up and down, ready for another go. 'Mountains!' he cried out, fists pumping in the air.

The floor below the cage swarmed with bodies cheering him on. The competitors appeared in a virtual alpine forest. The wolf crouched high on a rock looking down on the tree-covered canopy. The horse landed in the valley below him, lush grasses peppered with pastel wildflowers. She quickly ate as much grass as she could for extra points. The wolf wasted no time on extra points, hungry for the kill. His howl sent virtual birds scattering up from the trees. The horse-woman spun round in his direction. Her trot turned into a canter and then a full gallop; veins popped out of her skin, moist with sweat, breathing heavily and loud as she raced towards his voice. The wolf sprung off his perch, bounded over boulders and through trees, breaking branches and slicing a path through the thick, dense undergrowth of the forest to meet her head-on.

Mercy clutched the arms of her chair. Chase, eyes locked on the action, reached out and found her hand. She accepted blindly, squeezing his knuckles white.

The competitors screeched to halt as they came face to face, readied for a battle. Just as the wolf lept into the air, Mercy's PVA suddenly vibrated, startling her into a scream and jump. Chase and Joan looked bewildered. Mercy nervously laughed, pointed to her wristband, and excused herself.

Mercy, unable to break through the crowds near the front door, found the back entrance to the club. A dark blue light hanging overhead lit a vacant alley. Boisterous sounds of revellers on the streets nearby echoed along the brick walls.

'Hope, please go into silent mode.' A cryptic series of vibrations resonated from the wristband, deep into her bones, up her arm, and tapped her ear bone, creating a voice inside her head.

'Doctor Mercy.'

'Yes?'

'Lab PVA has reported results that warranted contacting you based on your instructions.'

'Yes, Hope. What's the result?'

'Your hypothesis returned a ninety-eight percent probability that mutation FFv1 genome did not evolve organically.'

Mercy went pale and shook her head in disbelief. A sudden fear squeezed her heart. She had to get rid of the study, remove her name from any association with the discovery until she knew who to trust. 'Hope, delete files from my database.'

'Complete,' Hope confirmed.

Mercy plotted. She would change the study criteria, so the results were not evident. Plan in place, she had to convince Chase to let her back into the secure unit.

'Doctor, I have other news on your health. Is this a good time?'

'My health? Yes, continue.' An instant thought of catching the virus froze her.

'Your daily medical scan revealed a zygote in the first cleavage. I can arrange further medical examination if you would like?'

Mercy blinked, shook her head, and fell back into a lean against the wall. 'Repeat that, Hope,' she commanded.

'You're pregnant.'

'No,' she repeated over and over again, in a shocked barely heard voice.

'Doctor, all fertilisations are required to be reported to the Population Control Centre. Would you like me to do that now?'

'Wait, no!' Mercy cried, unsure of her next move.

'However, you have the right to withhold reporting your pregnancy until the zygote attaches to the uterus.'

'You could have told me that first,' she replied angrily. 'Yes, please, withhold.'

'Very well. I will let you know when attachment has taken place.'

Random and rapid thoughts crippled Mercy. She thought of Chase and his reaction. She wondered what her hybrid child would look like. She thought of terminating the pregnancy before anyone found out. Unable to move from the alley, slumped against the wall, she kept shaking her head in disbelief.

Without notice, a sudden abrupt wind pricked her face, drawing her gaze upward. A blanket of black feathers engulfed her, muffled her shriek of terror. A sharp pain shot through her body as a razor-like claw sunk into her left shoulder, paralysing her arm. Another claw pried Hope from her wrist, tearing her thin underarm flesh; drops of blood stained the alley floor. Both shoulders under its grip, her entire body went limp. Slowly, her feet dangled, helpless, over the rapidly receding ground. A deep sleep seized her as she fainted.

Joan grabbed Chase's arm and rushed for the exit.

'What?' He whirled out of his chair and ran behind her.

'It's Mercy; her PVA has been removed.'

The large metal door at the entrance of the Orchard swung open with a bang, slamming into the back wall. The ally was empty.

'I'll check the street,' yelled Chase, already panicked.

Joan moved in the opposite direction. She spotted something on the ground. Bending down on one knee, she picked up Mercy's PVA.

'Chase, over here,' she called him back.

'Why would she take that off?' His voice became more and more desperate.

Chase grabbed the bracelet from Joan and brought the soft metal ring close to his nose, smelling for her. His nose pointed upward; his nostrils flared. Her scent was on the air. *But where?* He bent down and drew close to the pool of dried blood on the ground. He sniffed at it like a hound. 'It's Mercy's blood for sure. She's been taken!'

Joan summoned her PVA. 'Call Doctor Mercy's virtual assistant.'

Hope answered from Joan's wristband. 'Hello, Ambassador Joan. How may I help?'

'Hope, override privacy protocol. What's the last record you had with Mercy before you were removed?'

'We reviewed lab results, discussed her health report and then she was interrupted by someone in the alley. Her heart rate was significantly elevated. She screamed. I was removed from her wrist by force. That's when I alerted you, Ambassador.'

'Then what?' bellowed Chase impatiently.

'My scans showed her being lifted into the air directly over our current location. Exactly three minutes and twenty-four seconds later, she was outside my scanning bandwidth.'

'I've got to report this to the Prime,' continued Joan, already thinking of next steps. 'Chase, I'm aware of your relationship with Mercy.' She confronted him boldly.

He shook his head and shrugged his shoulders, 'And? You think I had something to do with this?'

'No, of course not. But I need to know, is there anything unusual about Mercy's movements or her actions over the last few days?'

'Not that I know. Other than…' Chase's voice trailed off, uncertain.

Mercy's stories about being visited by an avian hybrid, and now being flown away – he began to add the pieces together.

'Chase, other than what?' Joan commanded.

'She told me she had been visited a few times by a young avian-girl hybrid. I told her it was impossible. Avian hybrids don't exist. Right?'

His question should have been rhetorical. To his surprise, Joan deflected.

'We need to get back now.'

'I'm going after her!' He was defiant, peering into the dark sky as if she were still there, in reach.

'No, you're not. You have no idea what's going on. You're coming back with me. I'll send a search party out immediately. I want to know more about this encounter she's been having.'

# CHAPTER TWENTY-ONE

Tiny hands caressed Mercy's hair. She tried to wake herself. The delicate fingers gently loosened her wind-blown knots as she drifted back into sleep.

*Mercy hung on an edge, trying to not to fall into the endless abyss beneath her. Losing her grip, she plunged back first into the dark, watching the fading blue sky. She tried hard to liberate a stifled scream, but only silence came out.*

*Suddenly she was small, so small she could enter the High Chamber through a mouse hole. The stone floor cracked, slowed her. She ran, jumped, almost missed; they were leaving, the Five Leaders, they were walking away from the bench. 'Wait! I'm here!' she screamed in a voice so small it wouldn't even echo.*

*Cries, not hers. An infant was somewhere in her apartment. Why couldn't she find it? An animal scurried across the hall, brief, not long enough to see. A guilty horror struck her: fondness and repulsion in equal measure. The cries continued. She followed the direction of the shadow-hugging creature. The clip, clip, clipping nails on a wood floor, moved one room ahead of her, always in a never-ending chase. 'Please stop! I want to help. I can help!'*

*The cries disappeared. A bright shaft of sunlight through the window burned her pocket, reminded her of a note she had forgotten she had. Paper unfolded, she read the words: YOU'RE IN DANGER.*

Mercy suddenly awoke and bolted upright, gulping air as if surfacing from underwater. *Alive! I'm alive.* Her first instinct was to reach for Hope, only to find the scabbed surface of dry blood over a small cut.

Her surroundings slowly took shape. A million needles of pale light broke through the walls entirely made of a delicate patchwork of woven boughs, limbs, twigs and offshoots. The enclosure, curved from floor to ceiling, like the inside of an eggshell, was just big enough to hold a bed and a small table with one chair. Mercy was lying on a nest of straw and feathers. The sound of birds singing and hushed human voices were outside, intent on not being overheard.

There was movement at the wicker door opposite her. Mercy looked rapidly around, searching for an escape. There was none. She pressed her back against the wall in defence, causing a bolt of pain to shoot through her shoulders. She screamed out in agony. The door quickly opened. Daylight flooded her cage as she sheltered her eyes.

A tall silhouette of a man stooped through the entrance. The outline of wings arching over his shoulders called him out as a Chimera. Mercy's eyes adjusted to the light, and his face came into focus. Her capture was the avian hybrid that had visited her in Sky Park.

'What do you want?' she cried out.

The man raised a hand, gestured for her to be calm. 'Doctor Mercy, you might be a little sore. I've regenerated the wounds in your shoulders. I'm sorry about that, but better the pain than dropping you. I hope you understand.'

'Understand!' she blurted out, near tears, the pain in her shoulders starting to break through an adrenaline numbness. 'I don't understand anything. What am I doing here, and why do you keep involving me in whatever this is?'

'Allow me to start again. My name is Michael, and, well, I need your help.' He was direct, humble.

'You have a funny way of asking for it, kidnapping me against my will? Why should I help you?' barked Mercy, finding her anger.

'I'm sorry. But you're heavily guarded, Doctor Mercy. Many government operatives are moving around you. Getting enough time with you required these extreme measures.'

Mercy remained stubbornly silent.

Michael was forced to continue: 'Please understand, you are not in danger here, nor are you a captive. Once you've heard me out, I will gladly take you back.'

Michael sat in the chair, leaning forward with his elbows on his knees.

'The hybrids you know are bred to fit into society. To be labourers, scientists, teachers; to have families, even be leaders. But there are other hybrids – ones you don't know about, like me.'

Mercy sat forward, trying to find a more comfortable position and listened.

'There is an entire city of hybrids above classification 10, and new hybrids with avian and reptilian DNA created as part of a covert government operation,' revealed Michael.

'Why breed new species in secret? I thought the government's goal was diversification?' Her questioning was intent on catching him out in a lie.

'These new hybrids are bred with killer instincts – natural-born hunters who will fight to the death without guilt, remorse or question motive. That doesn't work in broader society but makes for a great military,' he said with contempt. 'By expanding hybrids to any animal DNA and allowing unlimited physical attributes, and you get a full arsenal: ground, air and water.'

A chill raced down Mercy's spine, causing a painful shiver of her shoulders. She thought of her initial meeting with the Prime, and an understanding passed through her. 'The Prime's threat to protect hybrids at any cost. She was talking about the military.'

'Yes,' he confirmed. 'The hybrid classification system is all about validating altruistic human characteristics, the parts of humanity that make humans feel good about themselves. Military hybrids exaggerate the sides of humans that are less admirable, even frightening: competition and aggression.

'So, we are bred in secret. Soldiers kept in a guarded mountain facility, trained for a future war, hidden until we are needed.'

'You seem human enough to me,' challenged Mercy.

'Some of us are born more empathetic. We are terminated if discovered. But some get through the system, intelligent enough to hide their compassion. I was one of the lucky ones, able to hide easily. Then I started seeing the clues in others, those who were questioning their purpose.

'When I realised I wasn't alone, I decided to help lead an escape. We've been on the move for almost three months. Hunters who've become the hunted.'

'The young girl who's been following me, an avian hybrid, is she with you?'

Michael launched into a series of bird calls. The door swung open, and the yellow-beaked girl appeared, wide-eyed, returning Michael's call with her trills.

'This is Jillet,' Michael introduced the child to Mercy.

The girl waddled towards her on yellow-clawed feet. She held out her small human hand at the tip of her emerald wing.

'Yes. This is the girl,' replied Mercy, carefully accepting the child's hand as if it might break. 'I should thank her, actually; she may have saved my life, warning me of a bear attack in the forest the other day.'

Michael whistled a message to the girl and pointed at Mercy. Her pink cheeks turned cherry red, a human reaction. Mercy looked fixedly into her eyes, tried to communicate a wordless thank you.

Michael sang once more, pointed to the door, and the child took leave.

'Is she your daughter?'

Michael pinched his brow, puzzled at the question. 'No. We are all sterilised.'

'I've heard that before,' Mercy uttered despondently under her breath.

'Excuse me?'

Mercy quickly changed the subject, 'She doesn't seem much of a killer to me?'

'No. Jillet was a planned termination, not enough killer instinct. But they kept her alive in the lab. It happens sometimes. Hybrids kept as pets.'

Mercy shifted uncomfortably; the idea of Chase and her baby kept as pets made her stomach turn.

He continued, 'I wouldn't have known about her, but the night before we escaped, she found me. I have no idea how, and I couldn't leave her behind.'

'I still don't know what you want from me?'

'The mutation of FossilFlu: it's out and spreading. We've lost a solider already.'

Mercy's eyes widened, and her mouth fell open. Images of mass death immediately came to mind. She had a sudden urge to tell the Five Leaders, warn them and all the people she knew back home. Helplessness engulfed her. She had failed to save them.

'I…I'm sorry, Michael, but I don't have a cure.'

'What was on the chip, Doctor Mercy?'

'Was that you!' she exclaimed, all the pieces of the puzzle coming together.

'Yes. It was me in the hallway. So, what did you find?' His tone was urgent, commanding.

Mercy turned her eyes to the ground, pensive. She considered her options. Instinctively she believed Michael. Or maybe she just wanted to believe in him, to have an ally in the crazy world that was unfolding around her. Either way, she confessed. 'The mutation is man-made,' she blurted out, feeling relief.

'I knew it!' Michael jumped to his feet, thumping his fist on the table.

'Wait,' Mercy found her own feet, feeling more confident. 'How did you get that report? It's highly classified.'

'You'll know soon enough, Doctor Mercy. For now, I need your help. We need your help to stop the mutation spreading. Can you trust me?'

Mercy reflected on his request, and all that might go along with it. She had already become a spy in a foreign country, pregnant with a half-man, half-dog hybrid, and now she was about to make a covenant with fugitives. Shaking her head, she wondered out loud, 'I don't know...'

The thatched door suddenly swung open. A sinewy winged woman entered. Snow-white feathers lay flat on her forehead, running over her scalp and down her neck. A shrill hawk's cry penetrated the room as she spoke. The quills lining her brow pricked up in concern. Something was wrong. Michael replied to her with an equally air-rending screech. The woman retreated as quickly as she had entered, having taken direction.

'We have to go,' ordered Michael.

'I need to get a hold of Doctor Chase,' cried Mercy.

'Not now, there isn't enough time. We have to go,' Michael repeated with urgency.

There was the sound of piercing bird calls and furious wing flapping from outside.

'Follow me,' he directed and ran out the door.

Outside, the air was fresh. The shock of light momentarily blinded Mercy. Her first instinct was to look down, to see where to take her next step, which elicited a terrified scream as she clung to the walls. Trembling, she realised the nest was on a branch at least five stories high underneath a dense forest canopy. A rainfall of leaves landed on her head as avian hybrids darted left and right, busily tearing the small treetop village apart. Vertigo forcibly took hold of her, and her knees went weak.

*Snap, whoosh, crack!* A half-man, half-scorpion, ran along the labyrinth of branches, slicing the vines holding the hanging nests with his razor-tipped tail. Nests fell all around her, taking branches with them, crashing into broken heaps on the forest floor.

Mercy gasped as a spotted leopard with a human face, bounced past her, displaying all the agility and speed of a wild cat.

A black bear suddenly dangled in front of Mercy giving her a start, his wrists held over his head by two avian men on a slow descent.

'Careful!' the bear barked upward as he swung quickly sideways to avoid colliding with a falling nest.

'Bird-brains,' he mumbled under his breath.

*Splat.* A white liquid fell on his head.

'What the…?' he growled, trying to shake a fist.

Hoots and caws came from a group of snickering bird hybrids overhead.

Michael swooped in on stretched wings.

'Be quick, people. Stay orderly and let's get moving.' He spoke directly to the bear hovering in the air: 'Amadeus, we're going north, to the caves. Let's gather everyone below.'

'Yes, sir,' the bear answered, trying but unable to pull his hand to a full salute.

Mercy, still clinging to the doorway, watched one by one as the nests around her plummeted down, cracking and snapping along the way. She nervously anticipated her descent.

The light disappeared behind Michael's ten-foot wingspan as he landed in front of her. 'May I?' He held out a gentlemanly hand.

Mercy wanted down, and any offer was a good one. She released one hand first, grabbing his with an iron grip, then slowly released the second. He lifted her into his arms, and, with a powerful thrust of his wings, they rose into the air. Mercy grabbed his neck almost too firmly. They floated to the forest floor effortlessly.

On the ground, littered with the debris of the treetop campsite, thirty hybrids assembled into an orderly semi-circle around Michael.

'The government has intensified the search party for Doctor Mercy,' Michael quickly explained to eager and waiting faces. 'We have to move. We'll be heading back to the caves by the base.' He paused, knowing that his next words would cause upset. 'There is more. I…we,' he glanced over to Mercy, 'believe the virus mutation is engineered.'

Audible gasps came from the small gathering.

'Why would anyone want to do that? It will kill everyone, not just hybrids,' questioned Amadeus.

'They can do it because the people who created it have the cure,' declared

Michael resolutely.

Mercy's eyebrows went up. *Is he crazy?* She suddenly remembered she didn't know Michael at all. What if he was delusional?

Michael continued, his tone defiant, 'So, we're going back in. To get the cure and release it for everyone.'

A reptilian woman with scales for skin and large gold eyes spoke: 'Thiss iss too dangerous. They are looking for uss already.' Her slim elongated tongue looped down and up over her head, tasting the air.

'Exactly. That's why nobody will be expecting us in the caves, so close,' Michael argued.

Nods of agreement came from some, and heads shook in disbelief from others.

'This is what we are trained to do. And I won't sit back waiting to get sick or caught,' Michael reasoned.

'What do we do when we get to the caves?' asked a wolf-solider, his ice-blue eyes wide and piercing through a mane of silver fur.

'It's a SeeSaw exercise. We'll be going in and out. Low key. You know the drill.' Michael shifted his voice, becoming more sympathetic. 'I know I'm asking a lot. Anyone that wants to stay back can.'

'I'm in!' Amadeus called out. 'We followed you out of the base, and it was the right thing to do. I'll follow you back in. For Tommy!'

One by one, the fugitives got behind the rallying cry. 'For Tommy!'

The corners of Michael's mouth curled upward as he nodded. A proud look passed over his face. 'Right, we have a plan then. Air troops will provide cloaking while we move on foot,' he ordered and turned to address a mole-man. 'Manny, scout ahead from below. We're backtracking so you can use the tunnel system already in place.'

The mole-man nodded, his tiny front teeth feverishly bouncing on his bottom lip.

'Athena,' he addressed the white-feathered woman who brought the warning. 'You'll scout ahead by air. Don't get too far; we need to stay close.'

The avian woman trilled and flew up and away, heading north.

'Let's get going,' Michael commanded.

Lasers ignited from small devices attached to six avians, connecting one flying soldier to the next, like a strung necklace. At the centre of the glowing outline, a dark cloud formed, casting everyone under its protective cloak.

The band of fugitives and Mercy started the long march north.

# CHAPTER TWENTY-TWO

The debriefing seemed more of an interrogation. Chase expected all the Prime's people to be on the case, a top priority, chasing the abduction of their first foreign visitor in living times. But things were relatively quiet considering.

A single search party was launched immediately on Joan's request, as she promised. But that was the extent of the international crisis. When the Prime herself joined the debrief, Chase demanded to know why Mercy's disappearance wasn't being treated as a higher priority.

'Rest assured, Doctor Chase, we have our best on it. The entire country is under surveillance. They can't hide for long,' the Prime answered with a note of irritation in her voice.

A profound moment of silence sat between them. The Prime stared at Chase as if she was trying to read his mind – to catch him in a lie before he spoke it. Chase held her glare, unmoved, confident he had nothing to hide.

'I believe,' continued the Prime stitching her brow quizzically, 'there are protocols around live testing of viral samples. Correct?'

Chase sat back in his chair, looking caught. He knew where her question was leading. 'Yes, several,' he answered.

'What was Doctor Mercy looking for that was so urgent she was allowed to bypass every single prerequisite for live testing?'

Chase let out a long sigh and shrugged his shoulders. 'Honestly, I don't know. And I should. But I had nothing to do with her disappearance, and I trust Mercy. She's the victim here.' His tone humble and imploring.

'You trust her because you slept with her?' the Prime asked, pinning him in a corner.

Chase shot Joan a scowling look before answering the Prime. 'I trust her because she has spent her entire life trying to find a cure for this disease. Because she has shared all of her research openly, without hesitation. And yes, because I know her. I know she would only ever do the right thing.'

The Prime glared at Chase with one last hard stare and turned to Joan. 'Keep him under observation.'

The Prime left the room. Chase let his forehead fall into his hands in exasperation.

'Please, Chase, don't try to go out and find her or interfere with the search,' Joan implored in a consoling voice. 'Let us do our job. I will keep you updated as soon as we learn anything. The Prime wants containment and, Chase, listen to me,' she continued waiting for him to lift his head towards her. 'You're also under strict surveillance, in the event Mercy contacts you.'

Chase pinched his brow with rage-filled eyes.

Joan leaned into the table forcefully. 'If you try to find Mercy without us, I'll have to put you in confinement.'

Chase's lip curled up over his long sharp incisors. 'I'll do as I am asked,' he spewed out the words reluctantly.

In truth, he had become tired and annoyed and ready to leave. Throughout the interrogation, he kept thinking about something Hope said. Something about sharing the results from Mercy's lab work. He had already made the connection between the report and the timing of kidnapping, long before the Prime questioned him. He needed to get to the answers before her. He needed to protect Mercy.

The early morning sun bled into the lobby of the living quarters. Chase hurried through the empty seating area, fighting back a yawn. He refused to give in to tiredness with Mercy still missing.

Back in the privacy of his apartment, he called on his PVA. 'Deox, pull all work registered to Doctor Mercy.'

'I'm sorry, Doctor Chase, but her work was classified above your level by the Prime's office about two hours ago.'

'What? But I'm the head of the Department on Population,' barked Chase, frustrated.

'Would you like me to request declassification?' asked Deox.

'No,' growled Chase.

*Think, Chase!* He barked at himself. *What was so urgent in the lab results that required her to leave the club? And what else did Hope mention? Something about a medical report?*

If he couldn't access her reports, he would find a way into the lab. He stormed out of his apartment, determined to break through any further barriers put in his way.

Two guards stood directly in front of the entrance to the Infectious Disease Facility. The guard on the right of the door spoke something in a voice low enough Chase couldn't hear, but he guessed. They had orders to stop him. He rammed towards the men, hands rolled into fists of iron, preparing to get through with brute force.

The sudden sound of the elevator door opening behind him broke his stride and caused him to hesitate. He turned. Joan walked off the elevator; laser gun pointed directly at his chest.

'Don't try to stop me, Joan!' roared Chase.

Joan dropped her gun, pointing the nose towards the ground.

'Okay, he can go through,' she told the security guards.

'What's going on?' Chase was genuinely confused.

'I've convinced the Prime you're an asset to the investigation – my asset.' She spoke her next words slowly, deliberately seeking a commitment: 'Chase, are you my asset or not?'

The two stood frozen, face to face, a stand-off of will and trust.

'Yes, I'm your asset,' he finally gave in, speaking between clenched teeth.

'Good. Now, let's go in together.'

# CHAPTER TWENTY-THREE

The band of fugitives continued to move steadily north, invisible from the drones hovering high up in the atmosphere searching for Mercy. They had been walking silently for almost four hours when Amadeus stepped out of line, allowing the troops to march past him. As Mercy drew closer, his eyes remained on her.

Well above C10, Amadeus appeared more like an animal walking on two legs than human. Brown shaggy fur covered his body, particularly expressive around his face where the coarse hair fanned out and backwards off an elongated snout. Mercy noted his opposable thumbs, one of his few human expressions. His razor-sharp nails gave Mercy a phantom pain in her chest where the bear in the forest had sliced her flesh. She wanted to reach up, cover herself in protection, but held back.

'May I walk with you?' he requested, his intent soft.

Mercy shrugged her shoulders and nodded. They walked in silence for several paces before he spoke again.

'I know about the attack in the forest,' he said bluntly, his bass voice soothing.

Blood rushed to Mercy's face. He must have been able to sense her nervousness. She offered a polite nod, but no response.

He continued: 'It must be hard – separating us from them, wild animals. I know it's different in the city. Well, I've been told, anyway. Hybrids treated like people. But where I was raised, humans and hybrids are not equal. Hybrids are disposable.'

Mercy broke her silence, feeling compelled to respond. 'I'm sorry. It sounds difficult.'

He turned, meeting her eyes. 'This is how it is. Nothing to be done about that now. All we can do is change the outcome; what will be.'

His wisdom surprised her, made him more human, less terrifying.

'I just meant, you're all brave,' consoled Mercy.

'I had a friend at the camp — a wolf hybrid. We were at the top of our class: best kill record and all. One night, during field exercises, we were separated from the troop, part of isolation survival training. He kept a watch out while I rested. I laid nearby, my back to him, but I couldn't sleep. I could feel his eyes on me, or maybe I just hoped. When I turned and saw his face, his wanting, I suddenly felt the same. We mated and lay together until the sun rose.'

Amadeus told his story with no filters, no sense of embarrassment, just facts.

'That was Tommy?' asked Mercy, remembering his chant when Michael called the troops to head back north.

'Yes,' he replied, eyes cast down towards his feet, a deep sadness settled into his face. 'Funny now, when I think about it – it was love, wasn't it? Attachment, at least. I guess. But Tommy, I think he knew more than me. I think he knew his feelings were love.'

'Where is Tommy?' Mercy asked.

Amadeus' eyes glazed over. 'Caught, taken to the incinerator.'

An audible gasp left Mercy before she could catch it.

'He wrote poetry –' Amadeus continued in a voice so mournful, so desperate and sad, Mercy felt her eyes grow wet, '– for me. Although he never used my name. A single expression of passion was enough to make him redundant.'

'I'm so sorry,' Mercy offered, almost near tears for the bear and his lover.

'You see, Doctor Mercy.' He looked ahead at the marching hybrids before them. 'Escaping is not bravery. This is what we are trained to do. But we have no training in living a human life. That's what scares us. We just want a chance to try.'

Mercy thought about Chase. Either by circumstance or design, Amadeus saw himself as an animal with human traits; Chase, a human with animal characteristics. And now she was carrying a hybrid child. What kind of future would it have? Would it be allowed to love? Would it be allowed to explore and choose its path in life?

Michael came to an abrupt stop, as did the troops behind him, almost simultaneously. Mercy nearly slammed into Jillet who kept close by her throughout the day. They arrived at the edge of the forest. A long valley stretched out before them, and the mountains were in sight. Mercy recognised the black stone ridge and snow-covered peaks from her trip north with Chase and Joan.

There was a shuffle in the treetops. Athena's white wings brought her to the ground, and she sang to Michael. He called Amadeus to the front. The three counselled in private, backs to the crowd. Michael turned to face eager eyes.

'We camp here for the night.' His order short and unexplained.

The band of fugitives scurried about the forest floor collecting branches to build a concealed camp, a practised ritual they all knew well.

Michael made his way to a nearby river. Mercy waited a moment and then followed him. He knelt on the silt bank and cupping his hands together, scooped up the ice-cold water, and let it pour down his head to his wingtips.

Mercy cleared her throat. Turning, he gave his wings a shake causing an explosion of water beads to rain down around him.

'Why did we stop?' she asked, her eyes on his, trying not to wander down his wet feathered chest.

'There is a lot of traffic overhead looking for us. We'll pick up again tomorrow.'

Mercy took a moment, then spoke again. 'Michael, these people seem to think I can help. And you seem to think the impossible – that there is a cure. What exactly do you know?'

His drying feathers flickered in the breeze. He spoke softly. 'They wouldn't have created a biological weapon without the cure; too risky,' he said, unapologetic for his earlier lie. 'We just need to get inside and find it.'

Her eyes shifted away. She had to think before she spoke. Michael's plan suddenly felt very haphazard. Of course, it made sense that if they had created the mutation, they would be trying to find a cure, but it was still a big gamble to assume they had achieved it. To risk his life, the lives of the people with him, and her life – all on a hunch. She couldn't reconcile that level of irresponsibility with the man before her, the man who had led a mutiny of soldiers to freedom. She could only conclude that he was hiding something; he must know more than he was sharing.

'How did you get that research report you gave me? I need to know who you're working with if you want my help,' insisted Mercy.

He met her stare head-on. 'Not now. Later tonight, when we have more time.'

Mercy nodded agreement, not having any other choice. 'Tonight then. So, how can I help with the camp?'

# CHAPTER TWENTY-FOUR

The Infectious Disease lab had been cleared of all personnel. The virtual display lit up.

'Playback yesterday's events from the moment Doctor Mercy's session started,' Chase ordered.

'That information is now classified,' the lab PVA instructed.

Chase clenched his fists and ground his teeth in rage. He looked at Joan. 'Why am I being locked out?'

Joan spoke urgently, 'I've managed to get you fifteen minutes in here. Use them quickly.' She ordered the lab PVA: 'Lab, security clearance approved, declassify Doctor Mercy's reports for Doctor Chase.'

'Yes, Ambassador Joan.'

The observation room lit up and began to play the recording of the events requested. At the centre of the room appeared a virtual Doctor Mercy, preparing for her tests with the raccoon assistant. The image caused Chase to yearn for Mercy, for his pack. He held back an urge to howl, something he had learned to control years ago.

Chase waved his hand, scrubbing through the video, gathering the highlights. Streaks of Mercy's image moving in fast forward blurred across the display screen. Chase paused on specific moments, examining her work in detail. At times he seemed lost, unable to keep up with her process.

'She's good. This would have taken my team weeks,' Chase said almost enviously.

He scrolled faster; the scene sped forward. He reached the point where Mercy's image prepared to leave the lab. At fourteen minutes into the video playback, with one minute left, it finally dawned on him what she was looking for and why.

'Good God,' exclaimed Chase.

'What?' Joan nearly jumped.

Chase turned to her, pale. 'She's testing the mutation for anomalies.'

'What kind of anomalies?'

'Human-engineered anomalies,' he said, sober.

'He was right,' Joan declared to herself, not revealing who *he* was.

Chase grabbed her by the arm. 'What's going on?'

'We have to get out of here, now! We're both in danger.' Joan's tone was urgent and almost afraid.

'Not until you tell me what is happening.'

'Chase, we have one minute before they realise we are here. I didn't get the Prime's approval as I said. We are both breaking the law.'

'Where is Mercy?' His grip tightened.

'I know where she is. I'll take you there. But we have to go now.'

He let her go. She pulled her laser gun from her belt and led him towards a concealed door into a back hallway.

Cautiously hugging the walls, they darted down the iridescent blue corridor. Joan in the lead, Chase staid close behind, more worried about her slipping away from him than his safety. They entered an emergency lift.

'Floor One,' Joan called out as the doors closed. They rose through the Earth's surface.

'Who created the mutation?' Chase confronted her.

'Doctor Brutus and the Prime,' said Joan, her eyes watching the rising elevator with anxiousness.

Chase twisted his face in shock and confusion. Nobody had seen Doctor Brutus since he was discharged from running the Population Research and Development Centre for his outspoken beliefs in extending the hybrid genealogy beyond C10.

'The Prime? And Doctor Brutus? But she fired him,' he said in bewilderment.

'Not fired. Moved. The Prime gave Brutus a secret facility. They are building an army of hybrids.'

'The avians. Mercy didn't imagine them,' Chase uttered the realisation under his breath. 'But why would the Prime build a secret military?'

'They are worried about the Purist movement. Senator Arjun has been ramping up pressure to shut down the hybrid program, and he has strong allies. The Prime wants a backup plan in the event of a coup.'

'That still doesn't explain the mutation. Why create a disease that can kill hybrids if you're trying to protect them?'

'That I don't know. I was told the virus mutated when exposed to the new hybrids. It was Michael who guessed Brutus was behind the mutation.'

'Who's Michael?' Chase asked, trying to keep up, not very successfully.

The lift opened. Joan looked around the corner, saw nothing, poked her head out a little further, and then darted out, gun swinging left and right. Chase followed. Nose held high, and ears perked, he sniffed at the air for human scent.

'Nobody here,' he confirmed.

Joan pulled out a new PVA bracelet from her pocket and said, 'Alert White Angel. We are at rendezvous.'

Within seconds of the command, Chase heard flapping overhead. The sudden sharp pinch of twelve-inch claws burrowing deep into his shoulders nearly caused him to howl. Holding back, he let out a muffled yelp of pain and grabbed the tough-skinned bird legs.

Joan's body lifted off the ground, voluntarily limp under the control of a white-winged avian woman.

'Let go, Chase, it's okay,' he heard Joan say before feeling his own feet leaving the safety of the Earth.

# CHAPTER TWENTY-FIVE

A north wind blew down the valley, relentlessly pressing down on the long wild grasses.

Michael stood at the edge of the forest, looking across the open landscape towards the jagged spires of the mountain range on the horizon – their destination. He turned and gestured for Mercy and Amadeus to approach.

'The overland is clear now. However, the search party covered this territory twice yesterday. We believe the next loopback will be in a few hours. Some of us will need to go underground. The avians will fly along the valley to the west, keeping an eye on the sky.'

'I'm not crawling into that coffin of a mole tunnel again,' stropped Amadeus.

Michael smiled, chuckling in disbelief. 'You are sensitive, aren't you? How you lasted as long as you did without being discovered, I'll never know.'

Amadeus scowled, embarrassed. He dropped on all fours, becoming a natural thing, nothing more than a bear in the wild. 'This is my cover. I can keep watch above ground.'

'Okay, that's probably better anyway,' admitted Michael. 'Manny,' he called the man-sized mole hybrid forward.

The mole-man's round, blubbery body, was covered in a dense coat of silky black fur. His oversized paddle-shaped hands with long curved claws were poised ready for service. He spoke from a small thin-lipped mouth below a raw pink fleshy nose. 'Yes, sir.'

'How far are we from the original tunnel?'

'About half-a-mile.' He pointed a stubby fat finger to the right, across the field, 'That way.'

'Is the ground loose enough for a quick surface tunnel?'

'Yes. If I start now.'

'Good. Let's get started,' commanded Michael.

The mole-man fell to the ground at the forest's boundary and started to dig, scooping up miraculous amounts of earth with each thrust. Within minutes, the beginning of a tunnel had formed, slowly swallowing Manny's head, then chest, until nothing remained of his body, only squirts of dirt shooting back out of the entrance.

Mercy suddenly understood Amadeus' reservations about crawling into the tunnel – the narrow excavation seemed impossibly small.

Michael informed the troops of the plans; all those who couldn't fly would follow Manny into the tunnel, arriving at the mountain caves by nightfall. Michael would join the other avians, keeping watch from the sky, and Amadeus would be on foot. If they ran into trouble, they would alert Manny.

One by one, the leopard, scorpion, snake and wolves, disappeared into the hole, crawling face first on their bellies, Mercy's turn drew near. Her throat went dry, and her feet refused to move. Unexpectedly, something tugged at her hand. Jillet was standing beside her.

The small bird-girl waved Mercy to follow her. Wings tucked tightly to her back; she disappeared like a rabbit down the hole.

Mercy was the last to crawl below the earth's surface. Daylight faded. The air tasted of iron. The thick smell of decayed grasses, weeds, flowers and dead animals crushed in damp soil seized her lungs. Occasionally she bumped into the wriggling feet of Jillet in front of her, causing her to slow down.

When pure darkness made it impossible to see anything, even her hands, Mercy's anxiety began to escalate. She swore the tunnel was getting narrower. *Keep calm,'* she repeated, only to find her heart beating louder and her breathing faster. She had to stop. Her head felt fuzzy. Panic gripped her throat, and for a moment, she was near fainting when Jillet suddenly started to sing. The short melodic tune had a clear beginning, middle and end, and then a start all over again. Before long, the metronome of Jillet's notes allowed Mercy to focus and breath regularly.

*Right hand, right knee. Left hand, left knee. Right hand, right knee. Left hand, left knee.* Mercy repeated the mantra in her head over and over again as she crawled forward.

Hours passed. But for Mercy, in the complete black of the tunnel, time was lost. The journey felt never-ending, and their progress slow. Impatience replaced her fear of dying. A massive root was no longer a snake. Loose dirt falling on her head no longer a catastrophic cave-in. And a crawling beetle over her hand was no longer an infestation about to eat her alive. Tiredness became her new enemy.

Mercy's mind began to drift. She thought of the foetus in her body, growing, becoming something like Jillet, something that could be treated as a pet by others. She couldn't stand the thought of it. Her stomach turned, and her eyes grew wet.

Suddenly, the line ahead of her abruptly stopped. Everyone piled into the person in front of them. Jillet went quiet. A muffled conversation took place near the front of the tunnel. Fresh air brushed past Mercy, and a palpable excitement started everyone moving again. *Right hand, right knee. Left hand, left knee.*

Slowly the breeze became a constant draft, and silhouettes and shadows ushered in first light. Mercy's face filled with relief. And her heart nearly burst with joy when she saw the exit, a single shaft of light burned onto the mud floor of the tunnel.

Jillet slowly disappeared up the hole. Mercy hurried into a sitting position. Her hands sunk into the loose dirt edge, and she pulled and heaved her body up and out of the earth with great pleasure and relief. She collapsed on the ground, face to the sun, breathing the fresh air with rapture.

Someone was talking. Voices slowly came to Mercy. She followed the sounds with her eyes. All of the fugitives were back together again and gathered in a small group.

Pulling herself to standing, Mercy looked towards the mountains. They were very near the foothills, but not as far along as they were supposed to be. Something must have gone wrong. She shook her hair, sending clumps of dirt spinning outward, and brushed in vain at her blackened clothing. Giving up, she walked over to join the others.

'They've released the wolves,' Amadeus told Michael.

'The air and ground troops are behind them as well,' confirmed Athena sombrely.

Izzard, the scorpion-man, spoke anxiously, 'But sending soldiers off the base could expose the military?'

'So now we know what's at stake and how far the government will go to get Doctor Mercy back,' replied Michael.

A sudden blood-thirsty howl wailed from the direction of the forest. The wolf soldiers were on scent, alerting the military troops to battle. They were close.

'We're not going to make it to the caves unless some of us stay here and fight,' announced Michael and pointed to the fugitive wolves standing before him. 'Shamba and Sheena, go into the forest and try to slow them down.' Michael turned and addressed the leopard-woman and the scorpion-man, 'Nila and Izzard, you take Jillet and Doctor Mercy to the mountain cave and hurry. The rest of us will hold the line. Manny, quickly, build a trench. We'll lay low and wait.'

An organised commotion ensued.

'Come on!' waved Nila to Mercy and began to run up the foothills. Jillet took to the air as Mercy, terrified, started running. Izzard followed.

The mountains were further away than Mercy realised. After twenty minutes of sprinting, she was out of breath.

'Wait. Please wait. I need two minutes,' Mercy pleaded, bent over with hands on her knees.

Nila stopped and turned. 'We can't wait. We have to keep moving.'

'I know, but I just need two...' Mercy broke off at the distant sounds of howling.

Down the valley, the band of wolf soldiers were now in sight and running directly at Michael and the fugitives, entrenched behind a new dirt barricade. Clouds of avian soldiers suddenly appeared on the skyline, followed by the loud hum of hundreds of drones. All at once, lasers lit up the sky as gunfire erupted from both sides.

Nila yelled at Mercy, 'Quick! They'll be here in minutes.'

Mercy spun round, adrenaline racing through her veins, and something else...anger. She screamed, pushing herself forward, her heart beating wildly.

The solid ground of the valley gave way to pebbles and stone shingles as they reached the base of the mountain range, making it impossible for Mercy to keep balance. Nila, dropping onto all four paws, bounced across the uneven surface with a speed and grace no human could ever achieve. Mercy gave everything she had to try and keep up.

In the valley, the first wave of drones raced past the avian soldiers. The deadly missles crashed into the earth barricade protecting Michael and his army. Dirt and rocks exploded and spewed in all directions on impact.

Manny lurched backwards. A fountain of blood shot out of his forehead. He lay still on his spongy back, eyes wide open, no longer breathing.

'Go! I'll hold the front,' screamed Amadeus to Michael. 'They will get to her if you don't go now.'

'You'll never make it,' Michael hollered back.

Amadeus grabbed Michael's arm and squeezed it tight. 'For Tommy.'

'For Tommy,' Michael called out and spread his black wings wide. 'Take care, my friend. I'll see you again.' His voice drifted away as he flew towards Mercy.

The second wave of drones had arrived. Amadeus grabbed a small egg-shaped weapon from his belt and threw it high. An electromagnetic pulse erupted from the device, causing the drones to drop to the earth, undetonated and unresponsive.

The military soldiers breached the barrier. The fugitives were losing. Amadeus jumped up from behind the barricade and threw himself into the fight. A wolf launched at his throat, tearing his flesh. He swung his right arm at the hybrid and ripped the creature nearly in half. Two more jumped on top of him, pinning him to the ground.

There was only one end; he had known that from the beginning. As blood poured from his open throat, Tommy looked back at him in his mind's eye. Amadeus had loved; he had known what he was never designed to know, and that was miracle enough if he were destined to die today.

Snarling, Amadeus let out one last booming roar and fought off the wolf soldiers, one by one, crushing their skulls and tearing their limbs before collapsing on his back. The sky overhead was blue. He took a long breath in and with one final breath out, whispered, 'Tommy.'

Mercy screamed as her ankle twisted on a loose rock and her hip slammed into a large stone. The sudden bolt of pain and the impossible angle of her ankle told her she wouldn't be running anymore.

'Go, follow Nila,' screamed Mercy to Jillet, who hovered overhead.

Instead, Jillet landed, unmoved by her insistence. Mercy pulled the young girl behind her, protecting her from the coming army. Nila turned and started running back towards Mercy but was too far ahead to help. Two of the avian soldiers were on top of them, hovering in the sky. Izzard, close by, glanced at Mercy's ankle and then down at the valley where two wolf soldiers were nearly on them. He took a position of defence, Mercy to his back.

Izzard was the first to shoot at the airborne avian soldiers. They seemed hesitant, held fire. He realised they wanted Mercy alive and tucked in closer. Within seconds the first of the wolf soldiers scrambled up the rocky slope, lunging at Izzard. He struck the dog square in between the eyes with his scorpion tail. The soldier slumped to the ground, paralysed by poison.

One of the avian soldiers took advantage of the distraction and swooped in for Mercy. Izzard anticipated the bird's attack and shot. The bird-man screamed, and spun to the ground, landing hard.

A second wolf soldier came at Izzard, dodging his tail, and pounced. Izzard's gun was knocked out of his hand and into a stone crevasse, making retrieval impossible.

Mercy realised the moment was upon them. They had lost the fight. An avian soldier flew so close to her that the air beneath his wings brushed her face. Suddenly, she heard a loud thump! The soldier shot out of the sky, dropped to the ground and skidded into a lump of feathers and flesh, his neck bent hard left. She looked up to find Michael's face staring back at her.

'I've got you,' he called out, sinking his talons into her and swooping her off the ground.

# CHAPTER TWENTY-SIX

The cave was sunless but not dark. Otherworldly inhabitants lit the damp cavern like a full moon night. The cold blaze of bioluminescent plankton, glow-worms, and fungi shimmered blue and green against crystal white walls.

Chase sat on a stone bench, face down, staring blankly at his feet. Joan stood over his back, regenerating healthy flesh where bird claws had pierced his skin. He barely moved…pain was the last thing on his mind.

'How is this possible?' he asked Joan. 'How could they do this without the public or Senate catching on?'

'It wasn't hard. The Senate doesn't fund the operation. The Prime does that alone. It slipped under the radar of most,' answered Joan, moving the medical wand from his left shoulder to his right as she applied stem cell lubricant to his open wound. 'Hold still,' she commanded as he twitched under the pressure of her hand.

'You said *most* – slipped under the radar of *most*. Who else knows?'

'A handful of Senators. Just enough so the Prime can continue.'

'And you?' Chase pointed out accusingly.

'Yes, and me. I've been the liaison between the Prime and Doctor Brutus.'

The constant hum of the medical regenerator vibrated off the cave walls.

'And the mutation?'

'I don't know what Brutus is up to, but whatever they are working on, it all started to fall apart when an infected hybrid with the mutated virus escaped into the Belt. Afraid the new strain would spread, and not having a cure, the Prime panicked. She had to find a way to reveal the mutation to the Senate

Health and Security Committee.

'I put together the scientific team who would "discover" the mutation. The rest you know.'

Chase pulled away from Joan. 'This all happened right in front of me. You lied to me about everything,' he accused her sounding more and more exasperated.

'Maybe, yes. But as soon as the Prime brought me into the plan, like you, I felt betrayed. It's not right what they are doing with the new hybrids. I started working with a group of soldiers on the base who wanted to get out and needed my help. The fugitives are the ones who helped us today and have Mercy.'

There was a reflective silence. Chase was connecting the dots.

'That's how the mutation got out of the base,' he said in a scarcely audible voice. 'You did it.'

'Yes,' she replied softly. Her guilt was palpable. 'Some of the fugitives were already tagged for termination. One of them had been infected with the virus as part of Brutus' research, but we didn't know. We broke him out of solitary confinement at the same time as the others.'

'The mutation is out? And they have Mercy…' His voice trailed off in a panic.

'Don't worry; she's safe from the virus. I've tested the remaining fugitives. The infected soldier died before he could join the others. He knew all along, and he self-isolated once out in the Belt.'

'But it can infect animals! Who knows what he came in contact with?'

'All the more reason we need you and Mercy working on a cure.'

'What do you plan to do with Mercy?'

'Brutus wants Mercy working on the base, helping him find a vaccine. Having her kidnapped was for her safety.'

'But her research is based on uncovering the existing immunity gene, not a cure. How will it help him?'

'We believe Brutus has bred a hybrid that is immune to the mutation, but he doesn't understand how it's fighting the disease. He thinks Mercy's research might unravel the subject's immune response and provide a cure.'

Anger crossed Chase's face. 'And you want the vaccine first. So instead of Brutus using her, you are.'

Joan sat forward, unaffected by his accusation. 'Not without her consent. She knows everything you know and wants to help.'

'Damn you, Joan! Why didn't you tell me sooner? We've known each other since school. I thought we trusted each other.'

'I'm telling you now,' challenged Joan. 'So, the real question Chase...what will you do?'

# CHAPTER TWENTY-SEVEN

Nila came to a stop on a cliff's edge and stood upright. 'Over there, Michael!' she called out, pointing west.

He saw it. Wings pressed back like arrows; he dove straight at the thin sliver of an opening cut into the mountainside, almost entirely hidden by thick overhanging vines. Mercy reached up and held Michael's legs tight, bracing for the collision. Eyes shut; she instinctively curled her body into a ball.

*Smack!* They crashed through the vines and tumbled to the ground, awkwardly rolling over each other to an uncomfortable stop.

Mercy cried out in pain, holding her swollen ankle. Nila was already inside, waiting. Jillet floated to a landing next to Michael, who stood at the entrance. The sky was clear; nobody had followed them. With a shake of his body, Michael shook the dirt from the cave floor off his wings. He turned his attention to the back of the cave, black and deep. Cold air pressed against them, pushing its way out.

'Joan?' Michael asked Nila.

'They are waiting.' Nila pointed down the cave.

'Ambassador Joan?' questioned Mercy in a shocked voice.

'As I said, you'd know who my contact was soon enough,' revealed Michael.

'That's how you knew about me and the report.' Mercy interrupted herself. 'Chase? Is he with her?'

'Yes.' His answer almost dismissive, his thoughts elsewhere. 'We need to keep moving. We don't have much time.'

The cave tunnel was black as a moonless night except for the glow of Nila's torch. She led them through the labyrinth of stone corridors by scent. Jillet followed, keeping ahead of Michael, who was carrying Mercy in his arms. After walking for nearly twenty minutes, the cave started to lighten, and their pace picked up. Mercy thought she heard the echo of a conversation. The voices grew louder as they moved towards the light.

'Chase?' Mercy cried out.

'Mercy!' came the reply and sounds of running.

Chase nearly slammed into Michael as he careened around the corner. His eyes fell immediately on Mercy, and his face lit with relief.

Mercy released Michael's neck and fell into Chase's arms, pressing her head close to his wildly beating heart. Drawing a deep breath, she lifted her face to look at him. His hollow eyes were weary but smiling tenderly.

'I thought I'd never see you again,' she whispered, tears running down her cheeks.

'We're safe now,' he replied, pressing his lips against hers.

# CHAPTER TWENTY-EIGHT

A new plan was forming.

Michael and Joan had pulled up a holographic blueprint of the military facility. They were deep in conversation about alternative routes into the base. Mercy's ankle healed under the care of Joan but remained tender. A sudden slight twinge of pain pulled her focus out of the conversation. Looking around, she couldn't help but feel the cave was only half full; Athena, Amadeus, Manny and so many more were painfully absent. They had given their lives to save hers, and now she had an unpaid debt, an obligation to do anything she could to get the cure.

Her thoughts wandered to her unborn child – a further unnecessary complication Mercy had to resolve. And she thought of Chase, permanently at her side since their reunion. She wanted to tell him about the pregnancy, but the words never came.

Chase pressed her arm and caught her eye. 'Where are you?' he interrupted in a soft voice, falling below the current of more important conversations surrounding them.

'Nowhere.' She smiled gently, guilt clutching at her heart.

He reached out and held her hand. The flesh of his padded palm warmed hers.

'There is no choice. Mercy and Chase need to go back to the city.' Joan said with decision.

Suddenly back in the conversation, Mercy snapped, 'What? I'm not going back. We have to get into the base to find the immune hybrid.'

'Joan is right,' Michael agreed. 'We don't have enough backup. Even if we get in, we'll never get out.'

'Going back to the city is our only chance,' Joan explained. 'Right now, the Prime thinks Mercy is here against her will. I'll tell her the fugitives found out about Mercy's relationship with Chase after they kidnapped her. They contacted Chase knowing he had direct access to the Prime, and offered an exchange: Mercy for military prisoners.' The idea seemed more plausible as she spoke it out loud.

'And how will that help?' Chase questioned, unconvinced. 'If we go back, how do we access the military base? And what about Mercy's safety?'

'There is nothing to hide anymore. You both know about the base so you can plead with the Prime to continue working on the mutation at its source. Convince her you're allies. Then we're in the facility.'

'It could work.' Michael sounded more optimistic. 'But, you'll need to win a battle to escape, and you'll need a prisoner as proof…you need to capture the leader of the fugitives.'

Joan shot him a horrified stare. 'No, Michael.'

'There is no other way. You know it. I need to confess to validate the story.'

'They'll incinerate you!' Joan protested.

'It's a risk we have to take. I still have contacts on the inside who will help me.'

Mercy stood up, her ankle feeling stronger.

'I can't let you, Michael. Too many have already died. I'll turn myself in. They won't want a scandal with the Sanctuary of Europe. If I tell them it was my idea, that I sought you out, they can tell my Leaders I enabled a traitor. That gives them the excuse they need to hold me here as a prisoner, keeping their base and the hybrid military a secret.'

'No, Mercy.' Chase sounded resolved.

He pulled her in, drawing her face to face.

'You have to get out. If all else fails, you are our only hope. You must go home and tell them what's happening here.'

'I can't…' she shook her head, unable to finish.

'You can, for me. For all of us.' Chase insisted.

Michael crossed his wrists. 'Ambassador Joan, I surrender.'

# CHAPTER TWENTY-NINE

All across Sanctuary City, PVAs vibrated and glowed red. Holographic displays flashed the words EMERGENCY MESSAGE. Confused and dazed citizens poured out into the streets and onto building tops looking up towards the darkening sky. Projected across the Shade, a large image of the Prime appeared, her face looming over the horizon.

'Citizens of the great Sanctuary of Americas,' she began, her thundering voice ringing out from speakers and PVAs across the city. 'When I took office, I did so with one promise – to protect you and to build a better future for humans and hybrids alike. We have accomplished much together. Our Sanctuary is stronger and more productive than we've been for over one hundred years. And we owe this to our collective efforts and speed of innovation. With science, we built the Shade. With science, we protected and improved our species through hybridisation. But this science can also be used against us.' She shook her head slowly and gave a dramatic pause.

'It is with great sadness today that I share this devastating news. Traitors are living among us. Those who would destroy everything we've achieved. Early this morning, our security forces arrested the leaders of the Purists party. Secretly, they had been engineering a new strain of the FossilFlu which can infect hybrids. Their capture came moments before they were about to release the virus into the public.'

Gasps erupted across the city. Citizens turned to each other in disbelief and fear, shaking their heads and clapping their hands over wide opened mouths.

The Prime went on: 'The Purists' desire to end the Chimera has never been a secret. Today we learned how far they would go to achieve their mad goals.

And I fear it won't be the last threat we face as we forge a new way of life for everyone. Rest assured, while I'm your Prime, you will be safe. Our way of life will be protected.'

Her face faded, replaced with images of the military base transposed over a rippling red, white and blue flag.

The Prime's voice continued over the speakers. 'Over the last few years, our government has been building a military in the Northern mountains. A new breed of hybrids, soldiers with specialised skills, who can protect our city.'

A scene projected onto the Shade revealed a parade of military machinery followed by thousands of marching Chimera soldiers, dressed in war uniforms, one hand pressed to their heads in salute, the other stiff at their sides.

The citizens shook their heads in disbelief; gaped in awe and confusion at the images rolling at them from the sky.

The Prime carried on: 'As I speak to you, the remaining Purists are being rounded up by this new military force. I will defend our Sanctuary at any cost.'

The image of the military parade vanished, giving way to a grid of twenty screens, all live video footage of avian, lizard, cat, and wolf soldiers chasing and incarcerating terrified Purist Party members.

Slowly, one scene expanded, eclipsing all other screens until filling the entire sky. An avian soldier hovered in the air over the White Tower with Senator Arjun hanging from his claws.

The Senator screamed out, 'Lies, it's all lies!' while desperately swinging his arms, trying to break free.

The soldier soared even higher until almost every citizen could see both the video and the real battle unfolding overhead. With one claw still firmly in the flailing Senator's shoulder, and the other now wrapped around his skull, the soldier twisted and stretched his captive's flesh and bones.

The Senator shrieked in pain, scraping desperately at the razor talons with feeble human hands. Then, before all the citizens of the Sanctuary, with one final wrench, the avian ripped the Senator's head from his body. Arjun's face stared lifelessly into the cameras, glazed eyes and a twisted dead mouth.

Gasps turned to screams from the stupefied citizens below.

Mercy sat alone in a room with no windows on floor twenty of the White Tower, dedicated to the police headquarters. Two chairs sat at opposite ends of a steel table with a holographic generator embedded in the centre. Leaning forward, hands clenched, she watched in horror at her private showing of the Prime's announcement and the beheading of Senator Arjun.

Separated from Chase and Joan the moment they turned themselves in, she had to rely on herself to get through the next few hours. Joan told their story precisely as planned and the Prime congratulated her and welcomed all three of them back safely, taking Michael away as a prize well won.

After hours of interrogation by officers, Mercy sat alone, waiting for the Prime. The holographic screen disappeared. Still sick from watching the horrifying event, she barely noticed the door sliding open.

'Hello, Doctor Perching,' The Prime's use of Mercy's formal name made it clear there had been a reboot in their relationship, back to the beginning.

'Madame Prime,' Mercy replied.

'You must be tired?'

'A little, yes.'

'I'm sorry we've kept you so long. These are extraordinary circumstances; extraordinary times, even. I hope you understand.'

'I do.' Mercy's reply was obedient.

'Such a horrible ordeal, your kidnapping. The fugitives didn't hurt you?'

'No,' Mercy shook her head in truth.

The Prime took a seat, relaxing back into the chair. A blatant attempt to draw in Mercy's trust.

'Doctor Perching, I believe we owe you a debt; a thank you at least.'

'Me? For what?' Mercy was on guard.

'Your research revealed the mutation was human-made. But, you knew that already, didn't you?'

The only way forward now was to play along. 'Yes, I suspected. But I didn't know who or why,' Mercy conceded.

'Of course.' The Prime nodded. 'Well, that's what led us to the Purists and uncovered their plot to kill the hybrids.'

Mercy's gut twisted as she thought of the Senator's head torn from his body. 'I'm glad my research proved helpful,' she lied.

'One question if I may. Did your captors ever mention the virus? Ask about your research?'

Mercy feigned surprise. 'No, why would they? Were they involved?'

'That's what we are trying to ascertain. It seems a little too much of a coincidence; your tests, the sudden kidnapping, the revelation of the terrorist plot.'

'I'm sorry, I can't help.' Mercy's heart raced, but her body remained still. 'We didn't talk about my research. We didn't have much interaction at all. They told me that if I behaved, I would go home safely in exchange for their friends on the base. I don't know anything more than that.'

The Prime eyed her suspiciously, her response measured. 'Well, the one thing we can be grateful for is your safe return. My deepest apologies for getting you involved in this mess.' There was a calculated silence before she continued. 'We've started preparing for your return home, considering the circumstances.'

Mercy's mind spun. They hadn't planned for this. She had to think quickly.

'Madame Prime, while I'd welcome being back home, we've come too far not to see this through. There is so much more Doctor Chase and I can achieve before I go back.'

The Prime raised her eyebrows. 'Are you sure that is the reason you would like to remain?' A crooked smile crossed her face, almost a threat. 'Ambassador Joan has informed us of your developing relationship with Doctor Chase. And we are aware you're carrying his child.'

Mercy grew pale. For a moment, she was almost faint.

The Prime dug deeper into her fear. 'You are aware we don't allow breeding for any hybrids above C8. I'm sure Doctor Chase informed you he is sterilised?'

Mercy nodded out of instinct, still numb with disbelief, the baby was never part of the story.

'Well, yours isn't the first "miracle". Nature has a way of surprising us,' continued the Prime, her voice almost annoyed. 'I'm sorry to have to inform you, but every pregnancy from hybrids above level C8 has resulted in abnormal foetal development. Most are self-terminated through miscarriage. A small few die shortly after birth. And in a few rare cases, where the parents hid the pregnancy, and the infant survived birth, the disfigurations were so severe and life-threatening that termination was the only morally responsible choice.'

Mercy clutched her stomach, fighting back her tears, not wanting the Prime to see her weak.

'I'm going to be blunt. For your good, we would like you to terminate the pregnancy before you leave. This isn't how I hoped to introduce Chimeras to the world, you see. The incident can remain between us. I don't think your Leaders need to know.'

'But it's my choice.' The words stumbled out of her mouth, surprising herself. 'I mean – our choice, Chase and mine.'

Terminating her pregnancy was always an option in her mind, perhaps already knowing it was the only one. But hearing the Prime make that decision for her triggered something she hadn't felt before: the need to fight for her unborn child.

Mercy went on, almost begging. 'If I chose not to terminate? See if the foetus develops normally?'

'It won't.' The Prime's words were direct, unhesitating. 'But, I'm willing to give you a few days to come to terms with this reality. And, selfishly, I could use your help. The man working with the Purists and responsible for the mutation is Doctor Brutus; he used to run the Population Research Centre. He's being held in custody at the military base up north. We believe he not only created the mutation strain but was also close to developing a vaccine.' She shook her head, a convincing dramatic gesture. 'Can you imagine the power that would have given the Purists if they had gotten hold of a cure?' she said aghast.

*Such a good liar,* Mercy thought.

'Doctor Brutus is refusing to talk. I'd like you and Doctor Chase to go to the base where I've set up a lab. You'll have access to his work. See if you can find anything useful.'

'Thank you, Madame Prime,' answered Mercy restraining her enthusiasm, a little stunned their plan seemed to be working.

'I'll give you forty-eight hours in the lab. Ambassador Joan will escort you to the base, for security. There are still fugitives in the Belt, and you're not safe.'

'Yes, of course.'

'Well, then, we have an agreement.' The Prime stood. 'We'll speak after you've been through his research. Now get some sleep. You'll be leaving for the base tomorrow morning.'

Alone, Mercy's face twisted quizzically; unsure who had just played whom. Her lips curled upwards. Joan's plan had worked.

CHILDREN OF THE MIRACLE

# CHAPTER THIRTY

Two guards stood outside Mercy's quarters. With no way to contact Chase, she lay down and reluctantly fell into a deep sleep.

Mercy dreamt of white-capped waters running down a river filled with boulders, forcing the water to split, twist, and push past the hurdles. A voice – no, it was a song – lingered in the air, brought to her by the cool breeze blowing down the pebbled banks. She recognised it; it was Jillet's melody from the tunnel. Mercy started running up the riverbank, towards the sound. Without notice, the location of the music changed, moved to the other side of the river. The crossing could endanger her unborn baby. Unable to choose, she woke.

Lying in bed, eyes open, a lingering sense of frustration haunted her. She tried to hold onto the images from the dream, maybe even fall back asleep and make the final decision, to cross the river or not. But the pull of the waking world was too strong. She found herself sitting up in bed. It was already morning.

Joan escorted Mercy to the docking bay and onto a transport ship where Chase was anxiously waiting. They sat in silence throughout the entire flight, hand in hand, no longer having to hide their relationship. Mercy caught herself daydreaming about a family, her possible family: Chase, their baby, and a new life free of viruses, free of politics, free of life-threatening missions. She brushed the idea off as silly, a waste of time, improbable. *There is no family, no life if the virus mutation spreads, she told herself.* She was a scientist, and a good one. Saving humanity, ensuring the cure for the virus was available for everyone – that's where she was needed right now.

They arrived at the base two hours later. The military vehicle slowed, coming to a soft landing on the roof of a large industrial building, a formidable metal structure with no visible windows from the outside. Identical buildings fanned outward from their central location, perfectly measured and lined up along a perpendicular gridwork of roads some forty blocks deep.

A concrete fortress, and the jagged snow-capped mountains beyond the wall, protected the base on all sides. Getting in or out other than through flight looked impossible. Mercy tried to imagine Michael and the fugitives escaping. The thought gripped her heart in sadness and worry for Michael, somewhere on the base if still alive.

The camp was busy in preparation. Armoury vehicles weaved up and down the streets, moving supplies from one building to the other. Troops of hybrid soldiers dressed in blue and grey uniforms marched side by side: bipedal hybrids in the front, quadrupeds bringing up the rear. Wings, claws, tails, scales, pinchers and raw animal muscle were on display in perfect synchronisation; all the armoury of the natural world bred into an unstoppable fighting machine.

The sheer scale of the operation exposed the Prime's real ambition. The base was not a military designed to stop a small political adversary. This machine was big enough to take over the world.

Once in the building, Joan led the heavily guarded escort. She moved with the familiarity of having been there many times before, passing quickly through security checkpoints, endlessly weaving deeper into the heart of the building.

She finally came to a stop in an enormous room, three stories tall. Layers of glass-cubed laboratories racked on steel beams, stitched together by a crosswork of staircases, filled the hall.

Bent over the upward rays of holographic light, dressed in grey uniforms, scientists worked in absorbed concentration, blind to the visitors entering their workspace.

'This is the Department of Science and Medicine,' explained Joan. 'We'll be working in the next room.' She pointed to a west-facing door on the other side of the hall.

Mercy listened half-heartedly, distracted by a peculiar experiment happening over Joan's shoulder. A life-sized holographic vision of a golden lion-human hybrid, with avian wings, sharp eagle's talons, and a scorpion's tail, roared and hissed, while the scientist prodded the creature. Mercy watched with both horror and fascination: crossing three or more species had never been done before.

'Good god; this is more like the lab of a mad scientist than a medical facility,' Chase whispered into Mercy's ear.

The angry creature finally struck back in defence. Venom squirted from its poisonous tail, bleeding throughout the holographic display like ink in water. Nodding in agreement with a pleased sinister smile, the scientist began running tests on the fluid.

The plaque hanging to the right of the door read: CAUTION: LIVE BIO-HAZARD MATERIALS.

'I have to warn you,' Joan started, in a quiet voice meant only for Chase and Mercy, 'this isn't pleasant viewing. All of the hybrids you see in these holographic experiments are real people, imprisoned in the next area.'

One of the guards waved his wristband over the security panel and the door opened with a loud metal clang and a smooth westward glide. Warm air, released from inside, pressed against them. A blood light fell out of the chamber onto the sterile floor of the science lab like a red-carpet invitation.

Inside, glass-fronted cages lined the cavernous hall. Behind the barriers, strange and ferocious creatures twisted and screamed, as they were prodded, cut and broken by the invisible scientists in the next room. Tiny black metal bots zipped along the cage floors cleaning up blood and venom nearly as fast as it fell and slipped back through the mouse holes in the wall, delivering the precious specimens for further evaluation.

Chase went white. A low menacing growl rumbled in the back of his throat as he spewed out his words, 'Joan, how could she?"

Suddenly, before Joan could respond, someone answered for her.

'Aren't they beautiful?' came the shrill voice of a tall, hollow-cheeked man standing at the door.

They spun around.

'Brutus!' Joan cried with surprise.

'Hello, Ambassador Joan,' his words slithered out, seemingly enjoying her bewilderment. 'And Chase, it's been a long time.'

Chase snarled and stepped in front of Mercy, placing himself between the two.

'I presume this is Doctor Perching you're hiding?' He pointed a gaunt crooked finger in her direction.

Joan interrupted: 'The Prime said you were incarcerated?'

'Annoying isn't it? These lies.' He sighed. 'You can let down the pretence, Joan. Michael has already confessed. I know Chase and Mercy are aware of my work. And I know what you've been up to, helping my soldiers escape.' He spat the words out maliciously, enjoying his position of power.

'Where is Michael?' Joan demanded, drawing her gun in his direction.

'Your gun won't work in here, Ambassador. And Michael, the traitor? He's right here as well.'

Following the direction of his beady eyes and pointed nose, they turned around. A dark cage lit up. Michael, chains clasped around his wrists, arms pulled wide, hung from its ceiling. His eyes were swollen shut, and his head dangled below his shoulders, chin to chest. His once majestic wings had been brutally removed from his bloody and mutilated back. Except for the faint movement of his beleaguered breathing, he could have been mistaken for dead.

'No!' Joan screamed, running towards his cage.

Michael, with great effort, raised his head and opened his eyes at hearing her voice. Joan placed her hands on the glass barrier, her shoulders trembling. Michael tried to hold her eyes, but the effort proved too much, and his head sank back down.

'Don't worry, Ambassador, you'll join him soon enough,' Doctor Brutus hissed. 'Guards, take her away.'

Two large black-winged soldiers emerged from the doorway and pointed their weapons at Joan. She turned at them, her face wet and distorted with tears, and raised her hands into the air without resistance.

'No! Stop, please stop!' begged Mercy, lunging towards Joan.

Chase darted forward to intercept her. Catching her arm, he shot Brutus a piercing glare and released a full, all-teeth, curled-lip growl.

'Now, now, there's no need for violence,' calmed Brutus. 'You and I need to find an agreement, Doctor Perching. We brought you to our Sanctuary with the hope that you would become sympathetic to our Children of the Miracle, help us find a cure and bring the message of hybrids into the world. We didn't plan for you to see all this.' He waved his hand across the room. 'And for that, I am sorry. But I still need your help. And after all, aren't we working for the same cause – to protect the hybrids and find a cure?'

'Not like this, not these hybrids,' Mercy shook her head.

Brutus' eyes grew dark and sinister. 'Very well, I have an offer,' he continued pleased with himself. 'How would you like to keep your baby?'

Chase's face slowly spun round her direction. She followed his movement with a terrified eye. Pale, his blue eyes clouded with confusion, he cocked his head, waiting for her to talk. A profound silence sat between them.

'What is he talking about, Mercy?' challenged Chase.

Her eyes pleaded for forgiveness before she even spoke. 'I'm sorry.'

'But it's impossible...' he stammeringly repeated.

'It can happen. It did happen,' Mercy continued defeated. 'I wanted to tell you, but...I couldn't see the point. There is little chance the foetus will survive.' Her confession spilt out in front of everyone.

Brutus cleared his throat. 'Excuse me. This is where I come in; or better said, we come together. I can help ensure your baby lives. The Prime wasn't fully truthful. Yes, out in the world, natural cross-breeding has never proven successful. But, as you can see here in the lab, I've managed to create all forms of life. I'm offering you a chance for your child if you choose to help us.'

Mercy's arm fell away from Chase. She stared at Brutus, unable to answer. A buzzing rang through her head as if someone had struck her with a heavy blow. How she hated this man, she thought, looking at him with disgust. But he was insignificant. The virus, her baby, Chase, her Sanctuary: these were the things she had to consider.

'Mercy, don't do this,' Chase begged apprehensively. 'Look at Michael. Look at all the people in these cages. What's their future? No, this isn't our future. Not one we should bring a child into.'

Mercy's shoulders slumped, and her eyes dropped to her feet. 'Okay, I will help,' her answer for Brutus.

Chase shook his head. His mouth hung open, uncomprehending. He stared at her as if he were looking at a stranger.

Mercy's eyes met Chase. 'He's right,' she continued in a private voice, meant only for Chase. 'The cure is worth it. I've dedicated my life's work to finding a vaccine. It's why I risked coming here. The virus is already outside this lab, and we are at risk, everyone. You said it yourself. We are not politicians. This is not our fight. If there is any chance the virus could spread, how can we turn our backs on helping?'

Ears laid flat on his head, eyes filled with tears, he pulled away from her.

'But I too have my conditions,' said Mercy shooting a burning glare onto Brutus. 'You will release Joan, Chase and Michael. Keep us here if you must, for now. Make it your personal goal to keep us safe while I work with you. And, yes, help me keep our baby. Then I'll do as you ask.'

# CHAPTER THIRTY-ONE

The cantina in the Science and Medicine Hall smelt of recently warmed food. Two guards, one wolf, the other bear, stood by the entrance, arms crossed, lasers at their hips.

Mercy sat alone at a long grey steel table; built to meet the needs of an otherwise busy dining hall. With a limp hand, she twisted her fork and stirred the green beans and carrots on her plate, uninterested. A fading twilight painted her face red; for the whole of the western wall was a window out onto a closed-in courtyard. It had been two days and four meals since Mercy had seen Chase or Joan. Each trip to the cantina she anxiously waited, even sitting long after her meal had gone cold, for one or both of them to join her. She was getting more and more confident they would never talk to her again.

A noise from outside the cantina ushered in more guards. Behind them, Joan walked in. Mercy's eyes lit up, her face radiated relief. Joan gave her a small friendly nod, collected her meal and took a seat opposite Mercy.

'Joan!' her welcome was almost desperate. 'I can't tell you how good it is to see you're okay.'

'Yes, sorry. I meant to come and talk to you earlier. But I've been taking care of Michael.'

'How is he?'

'His wounds have healed, but he's struggling. Losing his wings has shaken him. I think it will take time, but he is strong.'

'Well, you have each other. That's something, isn't it?' Her tone begging, seeking atonement.

'Mercy, I want to thank you,' she continued pensively, holding something

137

back, 'I mean – I feel I owe you at least that. You've saved both of our lives.'

Mercy knew what lay behind the hesitation in Joan's voice. It was the same disappointment that kept Chase from talking to her.

'But?' asked Mercy.

'No, but; I mean it. I'm just confused. Michael and I were ready to die trying to free the soldiers in this camp. Our friends have died to help us get here. And now this arrangement you've engineered. It's put us in limbo. We are alive, we are together, but we are more trapped than the people we were trying to set free.' She paused, then leaned into the table between them and spoke softly, 'Are we still fighting the same cause?'

Mercy glanced around. The soldiers were watching.

'Joan, the cause we are fighting for is the survival of humanity. How could I turn down the opportunity to see what Brutus has discovered and how I might help?'

Joan watched intently, trying to figure out if Mercy was lying. 'Have you forgotten what the Prime did to Senator Arjun? To Michael?'

'No. Of course not. But I need to know everything Brutus knows. Once we have that, the people and politicians can work out who's right and wrong. Not me.'

Joan reached across the table towards Mercy's wrist as if to offer a friendly gesture. She spoke in a nearly inaudible whisper. 'Mercy, who has the cure does matter. The difference is salvation or a weapon of mass destruction.'

Mercy nervously glanced at the guards out of the corner of her eye. The conversation was getting dangerous for them both. She pulled her arm away and quickly changed the subject. 'Have you seen Chase?'

'No. He won't come out of his quarters.'

'Should I go to see him? I wanted to give him some time, but now I'm afraid he won't see me.'

'What I know about Chase is that he doesn't quit. He fights harder.'

'Joan, you must try to get to him. Tell him to let me handle this and not to do something stupid,' she continued, refusing to let Joan break her stare. 'You both have to trust me.'

An unspoken understanding passed between the two women. Joan got the answer she had come for. They were fighting the same cause. She agreed to talk to Chase.

After a long day in the lab, Mercy ate dinner alone, but her eyes remained bright. She believed in Joan and deep down knew Chase would talk to her eventually. He had to.

As she was escorted back to her quarters for the evening by a wolf-solider, she thought about walking past Chase's room. It wouldn't be the first time. On two other occasions, she went out of her way to pass by, yet never stopped. He needed time, and her loneliness wasn't enough to take that from him, she told herself. And her palpable guilt made it easy to agree and keep walking.

Arriving at her room, just as her door opened, the wolf lurched forward and slipped something into her hand. Startled, she clasped the item instinctively and quickly pulled away. Before she could open her palm and look at the object, the soldier stepped back outside her apartment, took his position standing face forward. *Swoosh*. Her door closed.

Mercy quickly opened the piece of paper. The words read, *Tomorrow, breakfast*. Her heart raced, and a joyous smile lit up her face. Joan must have gotten through to Chase, she thought excitedly.

# CHAPTER THIRTY-TWO

Mercy was early for breakfast. Sitting at a round table for four, she waited anxiously. Minutes later, Joan and Michael arrived together. It was the first time Mercy had seen Michael since the horrible events of their reunion. His body moved naturally, healed, but his unsmiling face and sunken eyes revealed something still broken. The fearless warrior she had known in the Belt was missing.

'Will Chase be joining us?' Mercy blurted out before greetings had even been exchanged.

Joan shrugged her shoulders and raised her eyebrows. 'Maybe, but I can't promise.'

Just as she finished her words, Chase walked into the cantina, escorted by his guard. Mercy's heart leapt into her throat. She looked at him expectantly, awaiting his judgement, hate, scorn; wishing for compassion, encouragement, and above all else, love. He gathered his breakfast, refusing to look in her direction, until arriving at their table, where, for the first time, he met her face to face.

'It's good to see you,' she said timidly, hopeful.

Chase folded his ears back against his head. 'Yes, it is good.' His tone wounded but also forgiving.

He placed his tray on the table, moved the empty chair closer to her and took his seat. Mercy released a breath she had been holding. Her eyes grew wet; holding back an embarrassing urge to blubber.

Silence sat between them. It should have been a time of relief, yet tension hung in the air. Without warning, Michael's eyes lit up. He glanced sideways at the guards for the all-clear and spoke in a low whisper. 'For Tommy. Lunch today.'

Joan and Chase nodded, unsurprised.

Mercy suddenly realised the author of the mysterious note given to her by the soldier was Michael, and the message was not about a reunion for her and Chase. *Of course,* Mercy thought, Joan's easy submission to arrest, Chase's anger and distance; all of it keeping the guard's suspicions at bay. They had been plotting an escape all along.

Chase sensed her apprehension and quickly interjected. 'Mercy, I thought I would join you in the lab today. I want to help if you'll have me.' His tone not a question but a demand.

Their staring eyes crowded at Mercy.

'I would like that. I could use the help.' Mercy's unspoken answer was clear; she understood and would go along with their plans.

# CHAPTER THIRTY-THREE

Mercy and Chase were left in the lab. The guards took their positions outside the doorway.

Mercy pointed at the holographic display. 'This here, this is a test on an avian hybrid they asked me to look into yesterday. There is a genetic response to the virus I haven't seen in the other data, but nothing conclusive. I think this is when they found the immune hybrid. And here,' she continued scrolling through the data stream, 'this is when the test suddenly stops as if the subject disappeared. Or something worse...' Her voice trailed off, remembering the tortured soldiers.

Chase, his PVA submerged in the coherent light panel, spoke quietly and urgent, 'Joan has programmed your PVA to record your work into an encrypted file automatically. Everything you've been researching is on this.' He held her wrist. 'We got what we came for.'

'Did we?' she questioned his enthusiasm. 'This isn't a cure. I'm not sure if I have enough data.'

'Mercy, I've seen your work. You're a genius,' he encouraged her. 'Seriously, you have enough. We need to get out.'

A long moment passed. The heavy presence of something more important than their escape, more important than their own lives, couldn't be ignored. Mercy broke the stillness.

'Chase, I always planned to tell you.' Her voice drifted off. 'No, that's not true. I almost didn't tell you. Until the Prime threatened me, I hadn't realised that I might want the baby.'

'Might?'

'I don't know!' Mercy said, exasperated. She straightened her shoulders and braced herself as she prepared to confront his truth. 'What do you want?' she asked.

Their eyes for a moment met. Chase turned away first. 'I don't know. I never thought it was possible.'

An uncomfortable pause sat between them, neither having the final answer for themselves or willing to choose for the other.

'I honestly thought you'd never talk to me again,' said Mercy in a worried voice.

Chase placed his hand on top of hers. 'No matter what, you and I are going to be together.'

# CHAPTER THIRTY-FOUR

Outside, in the cantina courtyard, it was clear skies.

By one o'clock the facility had been cleared for the prisoners. Two guards, one wolf, the other bear, stood at the courtyard entrance. A further two avian guards stood inside the dining hall, at the main door. Everything was as expected.

Joan and Michael were calm. They were trained for manoeuvres like this. To escape if captured. To capture their enemies in return. They chattered about nothing important, unsuspicious.

Mercy forced herself to eat, her hands trembling. Chase couldn't stop grabbing looks at her; his knitted eyes worried.

On cue, the low metallic hum of the daily Solar Wave started. Clouds emerged, condensing out of thin air as thunder clapped in the distance.

One of the guards inside the cantina called out to the courtyard guards, 'There's going to be rain this wave; let's get them in.'

*Crack!* A slap of nearby thunder hurried their response.

'Come on, let's go, lunch is over,' yelled the bear guard.

Michael's imploring eyes alerted everyone to be ready. All at once, an ear-piercing boom caused a great fright. Confused, the guards instinctively turned their eyes up to the Shade.

'That didn't sound like thunder?' cried the wolf soldier.

There was another explosion, this one closer. Sirens shrieked from inside the compound. Giant plumes of black smoke rose into the sky.

'Over there!' Michael shouted, pointing to the smoke.

The bear turned in the direction of the black plumes, momentarily distracted. The wolf pointed his laser gun onto the guards inside the dining hall and with precision shot both before they understood what was happening. The avian soldiers slumped dead to the ground.

Michael had already leapt at the bear and was wrestling him, having the advantage. He slammed the bear's hand into the cement, dislodging his gun, which spun across the courtyard, landing at Joan's feet. Quickly picking it up, she tried to aim at the bear, but Michael kept flying into her sights. The wolf guard joined the hand-to-hand battle in a tightly wound ball of flesh and fur.

Weaponless but still full of fight, the bear growled ferociously. Foam dripping from his loose bottom lip, the bear swiped his razor claws across Michael's leg, cutting deep. Quick to take advantage of his gain, the bear used the ground against his back as leverage and launched Michael backwards into the air. The wolf soldier quickly stepped out of the brawl as if this was his plan all along. The bear's momentary victory was short-lived as the red laser of Joan's gun ripped his head in half.

A loud humming overhead cast the prisoners into a shadow. Something had come between them and the sunlight. A ship landed.

'Hurry!' barked the wolf soldier, waving Chase and Mercy to his side.

A hatch morphed open. Chase, with his hand on Mercy's back, urged her forward, shielding her with his body. Quickly, everyone jumped into the armoured vehicle, and the ship sped off towards the mountains.

Down below, in the open streets, billows of black smoke rose as mayhem tore through the compound. Soldiers started firing on fellow soldiers. Warships raced through the sky, their lasers blasting hybrids and buildings alike. Confusion reigned, providing a perfect distraction as the fugitives slipped through the air in the direction of the snow-capped mountains, unnoticed.

Safely beyond the base, but not yet free, the escape vehicle landed on a mountain top just minutes outside of the camp. The levelled peak ended at a cliff's edge and a sheer deadly drop to the forest below. An urgent disembarking left the four fugitives standing alone as their ship, and its pilots sped away. Five warships raced over their heads in pursuit, unaware their targets were no longer on board.

'Follow me,' ordered Michael and led them to a narrow stone path that wound precariously down the mountainside.

One by one, Joan, Mercy and Chase, threaded themselves into a queue, following Michael without question. Too narrow for a front-faced approach, they were forced to slide sideways along the gravel lip. Bodies pressed against the stone surface, arms stretched wide, hands nervously seeking and clinging to any thin crack they could find, they slowly made their way along the mountain.

Mercy's fingers started to bleed, and her legs began to wobble. Sandwiched between Chase and Joan, Mercy tried hard to match their pace.

'Keep looking up!' screamed Chase, encouraging her.

The path bent and curved, causing Michael and Joan to disappear continually, leaving Mercy to find her way forward. Tension ate away at her muscles and exhaustion threatened to consume her, but a glance down at certain death, kept her moving.

Someone was hollering. Joan turned her head towards Mercy and relayed a message from Michael, 'The cave is just ahead.'

Their pace picked up.

A black hole in the mountainside swallowed Michael, then Joan, and finally Mercy and Chase.

Mercy leaned against the cave wall, hands pressed against knees, and allowed herself to breathe again. Overwhelmed, she hadn't noticed they were not alone. A small, thin hand placed itself over hers, and there came a song she had heard before.

'Jillet!' she cried, grabbing the young girl into a maternal hug. 'How…what are you doing here?'

Jillet whistled and pointed at Athena, who was in heavy conversation with Michael.

Joan, standing guard on the cave's edge, was the first to spot the military ship coming at them.

'Michael! They are here!' she shouted; gun pointed down to the forest.

Michael and Athena rushed the cave's edge, guns out, bracing for a fight.

The slow rising ship did not attempt to attack.

'Is it one of ours?' asked Joan, confused.

'No,' answered Athena, still bracing for a fight. 'Something is wrong.'

The flying vehicle came to a frozen stance directly in front of the fugitives. A ripple of liquid metal shimmered on its side, and an opening appeared. Facing the cave and its inhabitants were Doctor Brutus and the Prime, backed by guards with guns pointing in a standoff.

Mercy pulled Jillet behind her.

Doctor Brutus smiled – the wicked grin of a winner who has cheated but doesn't care. 'Exactly as I hoped,' he laughed. 'Please, send the young girl over, and we will let Mercy go home.'

'What do you want with the girl?' Chase asked, confused.

The Prime spoke, 'Haven't you figured it out yet? The immune hybrid – the cure? She's the one. We knew the fugitives would never give her up. We needed your help in finding her.'

'You let us escape,' Joan blurted out.

'Outstanding, Ambassador,' continued Brutus, spitting the words out sarcastically. 'Now, hand over the child and you all walk away.'

'No!' shouted Mercy, getting more and more exasperated. Turning to Chase, she begged, 'Don't do it. We can't let them use her like that!'

'Think about your next move carefully, Chase,' argued the Prime. 'We need her for a cure. We all do. I've only ever wanted to protect you.'

Chase was silent for a moment. He looked at Joan, Michael and Athena; ready to fly into violent defence which would risk everyone's safety. He turned to face Mercy and tucked his ears back, pleading. 'You said it yourself Mercy,' he continued in a voice so mournful, so hurt and sad it brought tears to both their eyes. 'I need you to be safe and alive. This is the only way.'

Chase gripped Jillet by the shoulder.

'Chase, what are you doing!' Mercy screamed horrified and jutted forward, trying to put herself between them.

'Okay, take them both, and Mercy goes home. Agreed?' he said to the Prime, holding Mercy back with his free arm.

The Prime nodded and motioned for the guards to move in.

As the vehicle nearly mounted the cave's lip, Chase turned to Athena, nodded, and suddenly grabbed Mercy by the arm. Mercy turned her eyes to his. He looked down at her, pained, desiring, and above all else, determined to save her.

'Trust me,' Chase whispered.

Chase let Mercy's arm go and launched Jillet in the opposite direction of the ship. Like a hummingbird, Jillet's wings spread and suddenly picked her up. She raced away from the cave.

Joan and Michael quickly launched at the guards, opening gunfire.

Mercy, eyes locked on Chase, took a step backwards, off the edge, and fell. Chase held her stare, ears tucked back, eyes begging for forgiveness. A laser from the ship caught him and burnt into his chest. He sank to his knees, reaching for her.

'No!' Mercy screamed.

Slowly, very slowly, she was falling but never landing. A deep sadness made her forget the fear. She was ready to join Chase. Ready to hit the ground and die with him.

Something sharp dug into her flesh, wrapped around her shoulders. With a bone-stretching jerk, she suddenly stopped falling as Chase slowly disappeared behind the white curtain of Athena's wings. Mercy was rising.

# CHAPTER THIRTY-FIVE

A scarlet sunset bled across the sky. It had been two days since their escape and the horrible events of the last battle.

Joan and Athena stood on the white sandy beaches of the eastern Belt as Mercy and Jillet climbed into a small sailboat floating at the water's edge. No computers, no electronics, nothing trackable on board. Hybrid dolphins, now fugitives, circled the bow of the boat waiting to lead them to the volcanic island where Mercy's ship and Gia were waiting.

'You should arrive on the island by nightfall. Agent Basil has received the location,' explained Joan. 'You won't have much time once you get there. The Prime is already sending search parties outside of the Shade.'

'Thank you, Joan. For everything.' Mercy's tone was sincere but without tears.

She wanted to cry. She felt tears would show Joan how much she had come to care for her. How much she appreciated all that she had done over the last two days to plan their escape. But Mercy hadn't felt anything since losing Chase – nothing but ghosts. She lived in the memory of his touch, his soft pleading eyes, the warmth of his body, his breath on her lips. Oh, how she wanted to feel his kiss again.

'Take care, Mercy, and be safe. We are all counting on you.' Joan raised her hand in farewell.

A strong wind caught the open sail, firmly pushing the boat out to sea. Mercy watched as Joan and Athena disappeared below the horizon. Jillet, leaning over the boat's edge, fingertips trailing the water's surface, started singing. The melody drew Mercy forward, into thoughts of the future. The world still needed a cure for the virus, now more than ever. She wondered if she had the strength to start over, to find a purpose beyond her grief.

Instinctively, Mercy placed a protective hand over her belly and the new life inside. There was only one possible answer. 'For Chase,' she whispered.

# - END -

Children of the Miracle Series:

Book One - Children of the Miracle

Book Two - Oasis One

For more updates on the Children of the Miracle Series
sign up at: danielweisbeckbooks.com

Made in the USA
Columbia, SC
22 December 2020